THE
TURNAROUND

Enjoy the adventure and be blessed

Karen Robertson

KAREN ROBERTSON

ISBN 978-1-64028-739-6 (Paperback)
ISBN 978-1-64028-740-2 (Digital)

Copyright © 2017 by Karen Robertson
All rights reserved. No part of this publication may be reproduced, distributed, or transmitted in any form or by any means, including photocopying, recording, or other electronic or mechanical methods without the prior written permission of the publisher. For permission requests, solicit the publisher via the address below.

Christian Faith Publishing, Inc.
296 Chestnut Street
Meadville, PA 16335
www.christianfaithpublishing.com

Printed in the United States of America

DEDICATION

This book is dedicated to my good friend April Miller who read the manuscript via email as I was writing it. Her encouragement and urging to hurry up and send more new pages, kept me going strong.

To another good friend Jeanne Nelson who edited the finished manuscript so I wouldn't embarrass myself by sending it to a publisher in the raw. (Not me, the manuscript.)

To my husband, Barry who loves me through my creative craziness and gives me space to do whatever new project I take on.

PROLOGUE

BUS WRECK, TEN KILLED, ONE MISSING

Baker, California • Saturday, June 12, 1999, a gambler's turnaround tour bus carrying fifty-two passengers plunged into a ditch near Baker during a freak windstorm. Ten passengers were dead at the scene, three were taken to Las Vegas Memorial Hospital in critical condition, and one passenger is still missing.

The bus was on its return trip to San Bernardino when winds rose to eighty-five miles per hour, blowing dust and debris across the highway and obstructing visibility.

Bus driver Don Fulton stated that he was blinded by a wall of dust blowing across the highway. As he searched for the shoulder of the road, the bus jumped the embankment and careened down the hillside.

California Highway Patrol Officer Mike Turcell reported the extent of the damage and the great difficulty encountered by emergency responders who worked to extricate the injured from the twisted wreckage. The accident occurred at approximately 10:00 p.m. Winds did not subside until almost midnight.

The names of the victims are being withheld until relatives have been notified. A rescue team continues to search for the missing passenger.

Grace Partain read the headline in disbelief. When she left Highland, there were fifty-two passengers on the bus. They were all strangers and she planned to keep it that way. Now ten of them were dead, three were hospitalized, and she had to be the missing passenger.

CHAPTER 1

A Gambler's Special was far from Grace Partain's usual entertainment. An occasional bridge game with three other teachers was more her speed. Carol, Janine, and Fran had taught school with Grace for years. But recently, their conversations turned to griping about their grown kids and their husbands who worked long hours and made more money than they needed. Grace was tired of hearing these endless and useless complaints.

Grace's own situation was not much different. Her husband Phil was a successful real estate broker, and his business had grown to four agencies. Their home was plush, their toys were expensive, and their relationship was poverty-stricken.

Phil, a natural salesman, had earned his real estate sales license before he was nineteen. Along with property sales, he also managed apartments, which was how he and Grace met.

She had been accepted at California State University, San Bernardino, and learned that on-campus housing was already full. With no relatives living close by, her only option was an apartment, so she drove to Highland and began looking. Her first stop was the real estate office where Phil worked.

"Can I help you?" Phil opened.

Grace was pleasantly aware of the way his blue eyes traced her body.

"I hope so. I'm looking for an apartment." Grace was surprised to meet such a young salesman. His thick blonde hair was swept back and sprayed perfectly in place. An Armani suit and expensive silk tie broadcast his determination to be the best. Grace was impressed.

"Do you have a roommate?" he asked.

Was that a question a salesperson should be asking, or was it a proposition? Grace wondered. She had a feeling that her response to the question could change the direction of her life.

"Why do you ask?"

"If you're new to the area and don't have other plans, I'd like to show you the town."

Grace looked shyly away, and noticed the plate glass window where she could see her reflection clearly. Her short blond hair had a disheveled natural look that she could never achieve when she tried. The white tank top and shorts made her look younger than her twenty years, but she was still surprised at the offer.

"How about dinner?" She was shocked to hear herself ask the question. Color flooded to her face and she smiled demurely. At twenty, she knew what she wanted and Philip might be it. They made a date to tour the town, and in six months, they were married. Grace went straight through college and got her teaching degree while Phil topped everyone in sales and received accolades at every sales banquet.

After nineteen years of marriage, Grace's heart still skipped a beat when Phil held her close. Unfortunately, he had forgotten to do that for a long time. He often worked late and came home after Grace had finished correcting papers and gone to bed. Sometimes, he'd stop off in the den to watch the late night news and fall asleep in the leather recliner.

The den was really a trophy room. Plaques and awards decorated the walls and shelves. Sales and golf, those were Phil's passions. By the time Phil was twenty-five, he had passed the broker's test and formed a partnership with his high school buddy Sheldon Hargrave. Their annual goal was to increase sales by ten percent, and they always exceeded their goal.

The offices got bigger and more salespeople came to join them. Phil never denied Grace anything but time. Each house they bought was bigger and better. Phil was generous, and the gifts of jewelry got bigger and more expensive, but what Grace really wanted was children. Phil never thought the time was right and didn't take the absence of children as any particular loss.

"So it's no big deal. Some people just aren't meant to have kids. Guess that's us," he often stated casually. "Besides, you have plenty of kids at school."

At thirty-nine, Grace struggled with feelings of being unfulfilled, of living in an empty nest that needed babies, a nest where the rooster seldom flew in and the hen was ready to fly the coop. Yes, the children in her classes were hers, but only for a year at a time.

Phil made enough money so that Grace didn't have to work, but teaching was her life. She loved the kids and the satisfaction she got from encouraging each one individually and motivating them to set higher goals. Teaching wasn't something you got trophies for, but Grace was rewarded by seeing children whose lives she had been a part of grow up and become successful.

Phil's trophies represented time, money, and pride. There was no doubt that Phil was a hard worker, but their marriage was crumbling, and Grace wondered if he would work as hard to save it—or if he even knew it needed saving.

When Grace told Phil she had called to reserve a spot on the turnaround bus, he didn't seem interested. She hoped he would decide to join her, and she kept hoping until the night before the departure date.

"I'll be catching the bus in San Bernardino at six thirty tomorrow morning," Grace said as she kicked off her slippers.

"Six thirty…hmm. What time are you getting up?"

"I'll have to get up by five and leave by six."

Phil walked into the bathroom and turned on the faucet. "So what time will you be home?"

"I think we get back about one thirty tomorrow night, so I'll be in by 2:00 a.m." Grace knew he couldn't hear her answer over the running water, but he didn't ask again. When he appeared in the doorway, she asked, "Are you sure you can't come along?"

"No way. Riding a bus with a bunch of strangers sounds like torture. But wake me when you leave. I've got that Wilburn development meeting downtown tomorrow. It may be pretty intense." He got into bed and pecked Grace on the cheek. "This could be the biggest deal of my career." Phil shut off the light, pulled the cover over his shoulder, turned away, and was soon snoring gently.

Grace fought back tears. His work always came first and nothing she did had made any difference. During their nineteen years of marriage, the only vacations they took were centered on real estate conventions to resorts where Phil could play golf with other real estate people. Grace was capable of playing a decent game of golf, but the spouses were usually encouraged to entertain themselves by sightseeing or shopping, and too often, she found herself alone.

Grace boarded the bus with anything but a gleeful feeling. In fact, she really didn't even know why she was taking this turnaround trip except that school was out and she deserved some fun. But what fun would a trip like this be for someone traveling alone? She'd thought of inviting the bridge group or some of the other teachers, but they all had their own families and their own plans. Janine was traveling out of state to a nephew's graduation, and Carol was helping with her sister's second wedding.

To make things worse, summer wasn't the greatest time to go to Las Vegas. It was bound to be over one hundred degrees and she hoped the bus was equipped with exceptional air-conditioning. She planned to read and relax, trying to believe that would make her happy, but the whole twenty-hour getaway was really a pity party more than a fun trip. Grace was going off to feel sorry for herself, and when it comes to feeling lost and lonely in a crowd, Las Vegas seemed like the perfect place.

As the bus bounced along, Grace let out a long sigh and closed her eyes. The John Grisham novel fell to her lap unread. Taking a bus when her BMW sat in the garage at home seemed crazier than ever. A free bus, at that. What had she been thinking?

I'm surprised Phil didn't insist that I fly or stay a few days at some swank hotel. The class of people who ride the bus...

She surveyed the bus briefly to check out the clientele. Two or three people looked as though they might be homeless. When she had called in for her reservation, the woman told her there were a few "street people" who rode the bus back and forth daily just to get the free bus ride, keep cool, and eat a free buffet dinner in Las Vegas.

The majority of the other people were senior citizens who seemed to be traveling together. They laughed and talked like old friends who did this on a regular basis. It did beat driving and fighting the traffic.

Grace, who usually dressed in Jones of New York suits with expensive accessories, had donned a peach cotton pants suit and tennies in an effort to totally relax. It was really out of character for her, but these were the only clothes that matched her mood right now. Normally, she wouldn't go anywhere without first visiting the beauty salon to have her nails and hair done. Today, she had carelessly brushed through her ash blond hair and left behind the concerns of report cards, textbook inventory, and an unreachable husband.

As the bus lumbered along, Grace gazed out the window at the bleak scenery. Sagebrush and yucca dotted some areas. The rocky hills looked threatening and the desert temperatures hit a sizzling one hundred degrees by midmorning, promising harm to anyone who might venture out in it. For a moment, she wondered how long a person would live if they were stranded out there.

She realized that she was feeling stranded…lost in a desert.

The trip was uneventful. The woman in the adjacent seat slept all the way and only stirred to get up and go to the restroom. Evidently, she made these trips often and rested up for the eight-hour stay in Las Vegas. The tour hostess on the bus led Bingo games and tried to keep the passengers entertained. Grace was not entertained.

After the bus finally arrived in Las Vegas, Grace spent her time walking from one casino to another. She really wasn't much of a gambler, none of the shows looked inviting, and she didn't feel like eating. What else was there to do but watch the people and wonder what their motives were for being there? Personally, she was escaping the loneliness at home and finding nothing but loneliness here. The only difference was that here there were throngs of people bumping, shoving, and pushing by her on all sides.

When it was time to leave, she felt as though she had come for nothing and had accomplished exactly that. Climbing on the bus to return home wasn't any more exciting than when she first boarded for the trip. She hadn't lost anything, nor had she gained. She hadn't even carried on a conversation with anybody except the waitress in a small café where she stopped for coffee and a bagel. Even then, it wasn't a conversation.

The only thing Grace could remember about the girl was the WWJD bracelet she was wearing. As she left the eatery, she'd speculated on what it stood for. *Wynona Willamina Janine Dranfarb.* She chuckled. *Typical teacher, always making up word games. Why Would Jack Drink?* Maybe the waitress had a husband named Jack or John or Joseph. *When Will Joshua Dance?* Maybe her husband, Joshua, had always refused to dance. She chuckled again. It had been the only entertaining part of the trip.

Back on the bus, Grace settled into the front seat for the four-hour ride. Prone to carsickness, she made a point of getting there early to secure her spot. A man who looked quite disheveled and thoroughly inebriated fell into the seat next to her.

Oh great, just what I need. I'll put on my sunglasses and act like I'm asleep. She caught a whiff of her seat partner. A wave of nausea swept over her and it was all she could do to maintain. Digging in her purse, first quietly and then frantically for a mint or something that might calm her stomach, she felt the rancid taste of bile coming up her throat.

The man was already slumped over, fast asleep. With her stomach retching, she blindly staggered off the bus in search of the nearest restroom. Under normal circumstances, she would have realized there was a bathroom in the back of the bus. But a cold sweat seemed to drench her and the urgency of the moment scrambled her thinking.

By the time she reached the restroom inside the casino, the urge to vomit had passed, but she felt weakened by the experience. *Oh, the joys of menopause.* She had been having hot flashes that started out like anxiety attacks, and now this.

Grace chided herself as she regained her composure and walked back through the casino to the bus. *I should have told the driver I was leaving or asked him for help.* He had already counted her present and on board, but there were still lots of people missing from their seats. *I should have taken my purse! How stupid of me to leave it on the bus, unguarded. If the drunk is still asleep, he may not even know I'm gone.*

Grace suddenly found herself part of the shoving, bumping crowd again. "Excuse me. Pardon me. I'm sorry." The restrooms were strategically placed in the back of the casino so one had to go by rows and rows of slot machines and gaming tables to get there. She focused on the outside door and made her way swiftly toward it.

"Oh, my god!" A woman, clutching her chest, grabbed at Grace for support.

"What's the matter?" Grace tried to hold her, but the woman, who appeared to be about seventy, slid to the floor writhing.

"My heart…help me, please." There was terror in the woman's eyes. She hung on to Grace as she begged for help.

"Someone call 911! Quick! This woman needs help!" Grace's voice was a shriek, but only a few people nearby heard her plea over the din of coins jingling, change makers' inquiries, and slot machine bells. Some moved away and others closed in to gawk.

"Please…someone…get help!" No one moved. Grace felt panic rising in her. She remembered something from CPR classes about how to get help.

"FIRE! FIRE! FIRE!" she screamed. Almost immediately, a casino employee came running with an extinguisher.

"Call 911 and get some paramedics here. She's breathing, but she needs help! Quick!" Grace felt the familiar hot flash starting inside her, bringing drops of perspiration to her face and neck.

The man with the extinguisher pulled out a two-way radio and immediately called for emergency services. Grace sat on the floor and cradled the woman's head in her arms.

"Everything is going to be okay. Just hang on. The paramedics are on the way."

"Thank you so much for helping."

"What's your name?"

"Isabel…Isabel Hodges. What do you think they'll do with me?"

"I don't know. Is there someone I could call for you?"

"I have a son, but he's fishing at Lake Mead for the weekend. I doubt if he can be reached."

"Oh, my goodness. I forgot something…I'd better…"

Before Grace could finish her sentence, the paramedics arrived and took over. She got to her feet and turned to go.

"Wait!" Isabel reached for her hand. "Please don't leave me. I have no one."

Grace hesitated. She wanted to help, but she was anxious to get back to the bus.

"Let me just check something. Someone's waiting for me. Maybe I can talk to them about making other arrangements. I'll be right back."

When Grace reached the outside door, she realized there was no way she could discuss anything with the bus driver. The bus was gone.

CHAPTER 2

"Hey, Phil. Can you take a look at this offer before I present it to the seller?" Sheldon Hargrave didn't need to have anyone look at the offer, but he wanted to talk privately with Phil about something else.

"Sure. What's the problem?" Phil walked into Sheldon's office.

"I think it's okay, but I wanted to ask you about something."

"Yeah, what's that?"

"Could I camp out at your house for tonight?"

"What do you mean?"

"I mean Marilyn is ticked off at me and…it might be best if I just stayed away for a while."

"Did she kick you out?"

"Not exactly…well, yes. She went completely nuts over me missing her parent's anniversary party the other night. You remember…we were working like crazy on the Randolph deal."

"You mean she was mad because you were making money? What's up with that?" Phil couldn't understand how this was a problem. Grace never complained…at least not very often.

"Yeah, she kinda said that was the," he paused, took a deep breath, and continued, "the last straw."

"Ah, give her time to cool off and she'll be okay. Grace will be back from Vegas tonight, but I know she won't mind. Sure…come on over."

"Grace went to Vegas? Who did she go with?"

16

"I'm not really sure. She went on one of those free bus turn-arounds. I guess she just needed to get away."

Phil picked up the picture of Grace from his desk. He loved her in a way he couldn't explain. He was not demonstrative and found it difficult to express his emotions, but he was faithful. He had always been a good provider and had never been unfaithful…at least not in his eyes.

Grace hadn't been herself lately. She seemed edgy and irritable. He knew there was something wrong, but he hadn't had the time to delve into it. She wasn't sleeping well, he knew that. Every night he woke as she threw the covers off and later pulled them back again. Sometimes, he saw her just get up and walk around the room, flapping her nightgown. He didn't understand what was going on. Maybe this trip would help and she'd snap out of it.

It was late by the time Phil and Sheldon closed up the office. They arrived at the Partain home after 9:00 p.m. The house was dark.

"Huh, I'm not sure when Grace was supposed to get home. Seems like she said midnight or later." Phil shoved his key into the lock and opened the door.

The house was quiet and Phil cursed himself for not listening to the details of Grace's trip. Maybe she hadn't really said what time she was getting home. Or she might have said and he just didn't listen.

"Just make yourself at home. The extra bedroom is yours. How about something to eat?"

"No, thanks, I think I'll just hit the sack. I'm beat."

"Aren't you going to call Marilyn and let her know where you are?"

"I called her from the office, but she wasn't home. I left a message. Believe me, right now she doesn't want to hear from me."

"I'm Dr. Dornan. Are you Mrs. Hodges's daughter?" The doctor looked at Grace with such sincerity that she decided to let it go with a nod.

"Uh…she dislikes being left alone. How is she?"

"Actually, she seems just fine."

Grace was relieved but surprised. "It wasn't a heart attack, then?"

"We don't think so. None of the tests indicate it."

Grace remembered the scene in the casino. The frightened look on Mrs. Hodges' face as she gasped for breath, and her plea for help.

"We'll monitor her for a few more hours, but if she remains stable, she'll be able to go home later this morning."

Grace hadn't even thought about getting home yet. Isabel had been her main focus, for the moment. Grace had agreed to ride in the ambulance because Isabel had clutched her hand and fought every attempt of the paramedics to help her.

"Will you be staying with her?" Dr. Dornan asked.

"Uh…well…I…I don't know for sure." Grace saw no reason to go into any more explanation.

"Well, why don't you go in and see her. Maybe you can help her make arrangements to go home," he said, already on his way down the hall.

"Uh, doctor. Are there instructions about what to do when she gets home?"

He stopped briefly. "Maybe some bed rest for a couple of days, but otherwise it's business-as-usual."

"What do you think caused the chest pain?"

"We're going to run a couple more tests, but if nothing shows up, I'll have to attribute it to stress. Maybe she just needs some TLC from her daughter." He smiled and walked down the hall with his white lab coat flying out to each side.

It looks like I'm in charge here. Daughter, huh?

"Isabel, may I come in?" Grace entered the room where Isabel, looking small and helpless in her white hospital gown, gave her a wan smile. Her silver hair was tousled, but her color was back to normal and she was resting quietly.

"My dear, come here. What would I have done without you?"

"It was a long night, wasn't it?" A nurse had given Grace a pillow and she'd spent the night curled up in the waiting room. All night long, there was activity, constant noise, people coming and going as if there had been an accident of some kind. After being up since 5:00 a.m. the previous morning, she was too tired to be curious.

"It sure was. They poked me and prodded me all night. What time is it?"

"It's about 5:00 a.m. The doctor thought you might be able to go home this morning."

"That's wonderful. I feel fine now."

"You look much better, but you sure scared me to death last night."

"Well, I'm fine. Do you think the morning paper is out yet?"

"Gee, I don't know. I've been snoozing in the waiting room for hours. Want me to go see?"

"Could you, dear? I need to check something."

Grace went out into the hallway and asked a passing nurse where she might find a newspaper stand and was directed to an area near the front desk where there was a tiny alcove that served as a gift shop. As she approached the newspaper display, she spotted the headlines. In large letters, it read, BUS WRECK -TEN KILLED - ONE MISSING. She suddenly realized that the few coins in her pocket were all the money she had.

The sleepy vendor cut open the newly delivered bale of papers and gave her the top one.

She read the brief story twice in disbelief. Missing? When she left Highland, there were fifty-two passengers. Now ten of them were dead, and one missing. *Oh, my god, I am the missing passenger.*

My purse was sitting in the front seat. Why didn't the guy sitting next to me speak up about my absence? Oh yeah, he was drunk. He might be one of those killed. I've got to call Phil. He'll be worried sick.

Grace headed for the phones. She wondered how long it would take for him to notice she wasn't there. Search parties were certainly not going to find her at this hospital. In fact, they might not find her anywhere.

❧❧❧

Phil tried to focus on the clock as the sound of the TV jarred him out of slumber. In the other bedroom, Sheldon was trying to tune in the news with the unfamiliar remote and the volume on full blast.

Grace's side of the bed was undisturbed. Phil sat up in confusion. The sun was up, and he was certain Grace should have been back hours ago.

"…the name of the missing woman is being withheld until they can notify her next-of-kin. Meanwhile, three of the passengers are in critical condition and ten are dead. Only the debris remains to mark the location of this freak windstorm and tragic bus wreck. Live from Baker, California. Now back to you, Colleen."

"Hey, what was that about Baker?"

Sheldon was startled when Phil burst into the room.

"One of those gamblers' turnaround buses rolled over in a windstorm near Baker."

"Oh, no!" Phil could hardly form the words as the range of possibilities exploded in his mind. His stomach contracted and a ringing started in his ears. His legs felt limp as he directed them toward the phone and collapsed into his swivel chair.

Phil dialed information and asked for the Baker Police Department. After a moment, the operator explained that he probably needed the number of the San Bernardino County Sheriff's Department in Baker. His hand shook as he scribbled the number on a pad and thanked her. When a voice answered with "San Bernardino Cou…" he broke in without waiting.

"Hello, this is Philip Partain. I need to talk to someone about the bus wreck on I-15. I think my wife was on that bus. She hasn't arrived home."

"This is Sergeant Tom Childers. Thank you for calling. Let me put you on hold for a moment so I can get the file."

Phil felt a quivering sensation start in his stomach and run up across his chest, like uncontrollable chills.

After what seemed like an eternity, the sergeant came back on the line. "Thank you for waiting. Now, what is your wife's name?"

"Grace. Grace Partain. Where is she? Is she okay?

"I wish I had some news…but you see…"

"Is she alive?" Phil's voice grew louder.

The sergeant paused before he answered. "Well, I don't know."

"What do you mean, you don't know? Is she…is she…hurt?"

"I don't know that either."

"What *do* you know?" Phil's heart pounded and his lips quivered. "Is…Grace…dead?"

"Mr. Partain, the bus ran into a violent windstorm. When the CHP officer got to the wreckage, things were a mess. It was dark and there was debris strung all over the area. We are still trying to sort things out."

Phil tried to push away the morbid picture of torn and bleeding bodies and a mangled bus.

The sergeant continued, "We didn't even know anyone was missing until the CHP found some of your wife's credit cards strewn on the ground. There was lots of confusion. Firefighters and paramedics were tending to the injured. It took hours for us to be sure she was the missing person. I was just in the process of locating your phone number."

The image of Grace being thrown out of the bus appeared in Phil's mind. *How could she be too far away from the bus to be found?*

"Didn't you search for her or anything?"

"Yes, of course. But the wind was blowing like crazy and no one was sure of anything."

"She couldn't just disappear!"

"At first we thought she might have been disoriented and stumbled out into the desert. We've got a San Bernardino Search and Rescue team attempting to locate your wife right now."

"What can I do?"

"There isn't really anything you can do but...Wait! Do you have a recent photo of your wife?"

"Sure, she's a teacher and she has one taken with her class every year. How can I get it to you?" Phil's hands shook as he got ready to write the address.

"Just take it to your nearest police station and they'll scan it onto the Internet. We'll have it almost immediately."

"Should I come there?"

"No, Mr. Partain. We're doing all we can do right now."

"She's got to be there."

"I know, Mr. Partain. We've got a team in Jeeps and helicopters searching the whole area."

Phil gave the sergeant his phone number.

"Oh, and...Mr. Partain...please call us if your wife tries to contact you."

That didn't seem likely, but Phil thought the officer was trying to be encouraging.

"Please, keep looking, and call me as soon as you find her." His voice trailed off into a whisper as he sank into the chair and let the phone fall into its cradle.

"We will, Mr. Partain." Sergeant Childers spoke the words even though Phil had already hung up. There wasn't anything else he could say. *Where could she have gone?* The desert was a wicked place in the summer, but it just didn't seem possible that she could have gone far.

"Here's the paper, Isabel. It's quite a bit to handle." Grace had the Sunday paper cradled in her arms. "What section did you want?"

"Could you just find the sports for me, honey?"

Grace slid the sports section out of the paper, keeping the head-lines covered.

Isabel quickly turned to the racing section. "Oh, darn! Shredded Tapestry didn't even place! I told my son it was a long shot."

"You bet the races?"

"Only when Jerry insists. He gets a hot tip now and then," she chuckled.

Grace's father had been a horse trainer in his younger years and insisted that betting on the horses was like betting on rain-drops sliding down a windowpane. "I've always heard that hot tips were worthless."

"I should never listen to him. We never win, hon." She paused, thinking. "I can't keep calling you honey and dear. What is your name?"

"G...G...Gloria Franklin. I'm from Phoenix." Grace had never told such a boldfaced lie in her life, but somehow it rolled easily off her tongue.

"Gloria Franklin. Thank you so much for being here with me. How will you be getting home?"

"Well, I, uh…" Grace searched for words. "I flew over and was supposed to meet some friends who were driving through here on vacation. They were going to take me home. But uh…their car broke down near Lake Tahoe and they're stuck there. So I'm kind of stuck, too. I was just thinking about checking on flights when you fell in front of me." Grace wasn't sure why she was bent on hiding the truth for now.

"Would you consider staying long enough to help me get home?"

"Well, yes, I guess I could. Actually…I don't have a lot of choices."

"What do you mean?" Isabel's face registered concern and hurt.

"I did the stupidest thing. When you fell, I laid my purse and stuff down so I could help you." Grace lied again.

"I'm glad you did, but what's the problem?"

"When the paramedics arrived, I ran out to see if my ride was waiting, and I guess someone picked up my things because they were gone. Now I really am stuck."

"I don't want you to feel like you're stuck with me."

"Oh, I didn't mean that! It's just that I kind of made a mess of things."

"Nonsense. You were wonderful. Do you have a family waiting for you?"

"Uh…no. My children are grown. They live on the east coast. I'm divorced." Grace was getting the hang of this storytelling and enjoying it immensely.

"What about a job?"

"I just got finished shooting a documentary film on desert life and we're between projects." That was an unexpected whopper.

"I guess I'm stuck, too. I don't have a purse or any money either."

"Oh, yes, you do. You had an iron grip on *your* purse all the way to the ambulance. That's what made me think to go back looking for mine. I'm sure your purse is still here." Grace walked to the small storage closet and pulled out the white purse. "Yes, here it is."

"Gloria, you really are my hero. Let me see that for a moment, please."

Isabel dug through her belongings. She held out a quarter. "Could you call my house and see if Jerry is home?"

"Okay, but who's Jerry?"

"He's my son. If he's not there, just leave a message and tell him I'm in the hospital."

"Won't that scare him?"

"Ha! I wish. He doesn't pay a bit of attention to me."

"What if he doesn't get the message?"

"If we don't hear from him, we'll take a cab home."

Isabel nonchalantly reached for the front page as Grace left the room. She was bound to see the story about the wreck.

When Grace finally located a phone booth, she stepped inside and closed the door. She had no intention of calling Jerry or anybody else until she had figured out a plan.

So far, Isabel had no idea who she really was, and wouldn't unless they started flashing her photo on TV. They would have to notify Phil to get that. If she could keep Isabel away from the newspaper and TV for a couple of days, the news would die down and Grace would die with it. Phil wouldn't even notice she was gone unless he was notified.

Grace leaned her head back against the wall and drew in a deep breath. This was an opportunity to just disappear off the face of the earth. She could go to some far off place and take on a new identity.

Suddenly, she felt like her body was on fire from the inside out. Her chest tightened causing her to feel disoriented and lightheaded. She took a deep breath and tried to calm down without success.

Night sweats. That's what they called them when you were asleep. But now they were coming more often even during the waking hours. Hot flashes. There was no denying it. Perspiration poured off her face and neck.

When the anxiety subsided and Grace felt normal again, she punched in Isabel's home number. There was no answer but a man's voice on the machine asked her to leave a message.

"Hello, this is Gr...Gloria Franklin. I'm with your mother. She's in the hospital. She's doing fine. They'll be releasing her sometime this morning and I'll be accompanying her home. I'm looking forward to meeting you."

When Grace returned to the room, the TV was blasting out the story of the bus wreck. Ten dead, three in critical condition, and one still missing.

"Missing? Wonder how he got lost?" Isabel spoke as if to herself.

"Hmm. Maybe he got disoriented in the wind storm and wandered out on the desert." Grace thought it interesting that Isabel assumed it was a man.

"You'd think they'd find him easily now that the wind's died down."

"You'd think..." Grace opened the drawer in the metal nightstand, and noticing the Bible placed there by the Gideons, she picked it up. She thumbed through the pages absentmindedly until her eyes fell on the words, "...but Noah found GRACE in the eyes of the Lord." Grace flinched, slammed the book shut, and shoved it back in the drawer.

CHAPTER 3

Pete Jensen and LeRoy Ratcliff were regulars on the road between San Bernardino and Las Vegas. They owned a battered old tow truck and the desert heat, hard on car cooling systems, kept them in customers.

"They shoulda called us to help with that bus wreck yesterday." LeRoy spit a stream of tobacco out the passenger window.

"What the heck would we done if they'd called? I doubt we could right a bus if it was turned upside down." Pete's left arm was a dark dirty brown from riding with it out the window and neglecting soap. He always drove. The loading and unloading was too much like work so he tried to make sure LeRoy did most of that. Both men wore dirty overalls without shirts, and greasy baseball caps. Pete was so fat his belly pressed against the steering wheel causing a constant drag. LeRoy, tall and thin, seemed lost in overalls that flopped freely about his skinny frame.

"We woulda got paid big bucks to turn that sucker."

"Yeah, and it would have cost every bit of it to put our old truck back together after a tug like that." Pete absently scratched his hairy chest.

There was never enough money to pay for repairs to their aging truck and also buy enough beer for a party, so when times got too tough, the two men would tow a car or two whose owners hadn't requested it. They had friends out in a remote area that would strip them for parts, or paint them, or just transport them to another state.

Pete and LeRoy didn't do it very often because getting caught would have been bad for business. They'd both done jail time for petty theft, but stealing cars might land them in prison.

"I think that wreck was right up here by Baker. How 'bout we stop by and see what we can find?" It was the first idea LeRoy had had all day.

"Now, why in the world would we want to go pokin' around that wreck?"

"Maybe when it rolled over, some of them folks' winnin's got flung out the winda."

"Oh, yeah, I'm sure of it. Prob'ly just laying out there, waitin' fer us to come along and pick it up." Pete was smirking, but his brain was thinking this might be a fine idea after all.

"The least you can do is slow down and take a look."

"I'll slow down. If you see treasures a-sparklin', you just yell out, and I'll stop so's you can go pick 'em up. Ya think you might be needin' a shovel?" He threw his head back and guffawed.

LeRoy shook off the smart remarks and began to search for signs of the wreckage.

The two men had been together for a long time. As children, they grew up living on the same unpaved street on the outskirts of Barstow. No sidewalks or gutters, just dust. Through elementary school, they spent every waking hour playing outside, riding bikes, making trails, and getting dirty. Pete's father worked in a garage and had a bunch of old broken-down cars parked forlornly on cinder blocks behind their house. He was always going to fix them up and sell them, but he seldom got home before dark. His paycheck often was spent on beer with nothing left over to buy parts to fix the cars or feed his family. Pete had two younger brothers, so his mother stayed home and took in ironing to pay for groceries.

LeRoy, always small for his age, fell prey to the neighborhood bullies and Pete found himself constantly defending him. When they got into high school and got their drivers licenses, they fixed up two of the old cars in Pete's backyard. Drag racing after school was their favorite pastime. Auto shop was the only class they attended regularly, and that was only because they could use the shop tools to tune up their own hot rods. If they hadn't had to read the parts manuals and figure costs, they probably would never have learned to read, write, or do simple math.

LeRoy's parents were split up. He hadn't seen his father since he was six and his mother was a waitress in a trucker's café. LeRoy was an only child, and his mom wasn't home much, so he spent most of his time at Pete's house.

During high school, they both found jobs in gas stations and saved whatever money they could. On the side, they did mechanic work for other kids who couldn't do it themselves. When they saved enough money to make a down payment on the old tow truck, they quit school and hit the road. They both still lived at home, but considered themselves business owners even though they almost never made a profit, and were lucky to break even.

LeRoy saw the debris and tire tracks first. Moments later, Pete pulled off to the side of the road. The aging truck's doors squealed in complaint as they got out.

"Looks like things is perty well picked over." Pete kicked a rusty can and stuffed his hands deep in his overall pockets.

There was nobody in sight. The bus was gone and all that remained were the prints and ridges in the sand formed by metal being dragged, people walking around aimlessly, and emergency vehicles that pulled off the road to help.

"There ain't nothin' out here." Pete turned toward the truck just in time to see LeRoy do a hop, skip, and a jump.

"Now, what was that all about?" Pete asked sarcastically.

"I seen somethin'!"

"If ya seen somethin,' what was ya dancin' about?"

29

LeRoy squatted down and carefully lifted the heel of his battered boot. His crusty fingers grasped a piece of paper he had trapped.

"Okay, whatcha got there?" Pete walked toward LeRoy expecting to admonish him about picking up candy wrappers or some other worthless thing.

"It's a driver's license. How 'bout that?" LeRoy smiled toothlessly as tobacco juice formed a brown drip in the corner of his mouth.

"Well. Big deal. Let me see it." Pete tried to pull it from LeRoy's hand, but to no avail. Tugging back and forth, they both squinted in the bright noonday sun trying to read the damaged license.

Pete dusted the surface with his greasy fingers. "Looks like Gr... Partain. The first name's scratched off...must be Gretta or Grace... hmm...wonder if she was in the bus wreck."

"I bet she'd like to have this back—might even give us a little somethin' for returnin' it. Whad'ya think?" LeRoy looked at Pete for approval.

"Let's head over to State Line and see if we can call her." They jumped back in the old tow truck to another chorus of squealing hinges. After several tries, Pete got the old truck started and headed back on the highway.

※

It was almost noon on Sunday when Grace helped Isabel into the taxi. The whole charade was beginning to scare Grace. At first, it was almost like a childish adventure, but now that she had committed to it, there were more and more details to work out. She wondered how long it would be before her picture would appear on TV.

Isabel peered out the window, taking in the view as though she was on a city tour. Her lime green polyester dress looked as fresh as it had the day before. She folded her hands in her lap with the handle of her purse securely over her arm.

A stream of cars exited a driveway in front of them, causing the cab driver to hit the brakes.

"Zeez...church people! Zay alwayz een my way!" The driver slapped the steering wheel with the heel of his hand, and merged with the out-flowing traffic.

Grace gazed at the white-steepled church as they passed. She thought about the Baptist church she attended as a child. Every Sunday, her mother dressed her and her two brothers in their best clothes and took them to Sunday school. They had lots of friends there. Grace went to the girl's class while the boys went off to the class for boys. Dad never came along unless the children performed in a special program, and that was after much coaxing and begging. He'd sit in the back and leave as soon as the program was over.

It didn't bother Grace, but she could see the hurt look on her mother's face when he would drive off in his own car. He never even gave her a chance to introduce him to her church friends.

One Christmas, Grace played Mary in the Christmas pageant. She didn't have any lines to say, but the Sunday school teacher put some light rouge on her cheeks and told her she looked beautiful. A pale blue sheet over her head and wrapped around her body like a sarong served as a costume.

The narrator read, "...and they came with haste, and found Mary and Joseph and the babe lying in a manger." Grace was puzzled. How could Mary, Joseph, and the baby Jesus all fit in the manger? It made her smile to think about it.

But when she made her way down the aisle and out the front door of the church, she passed by her father. He was sitting in the back row near the door. Tears were on his cheeks and Grace wondered why he was so sad. Of course, when all the cast members had returned their costumes and she was sent to meet her parents, Dad had already gone home.

"Do you ever go to church, Isabel?"

The question brought Isabel to attention.

"Well, sure. I went to Jerry's wedding about twenty years ago."

"You mean you haven't been since then?"

"No. They got a divorce, and I never could see any sense in it. Why?"

Grace didn't answer but closed her eyes and remembered how much she loved being involved in the church. Her friends there were warm and friendly, and felt like family. What had happened to those days?

At first, Phil wanted to go every week. He shook hands with everyone and slipped his business card into every hand he shook. When everyone knew the Partains and he had cultivated as many potential customers as he thought necessary, he started skipping church to catch up on paperwork and play golf. Grace continued to go to church alone. She envied the couples who participated in small groups as they shared the increased closeness they felt after the experience. As much as she wanted him to, she could never get Phil to participate in any of the couples' groups. Finally, discouraged, Grace fell into the habit of planning her week's lessons on Sunday morning. She didn't want to go to church alone like her mother did, but discovered that not going and staying home alone was worse.

"Here vee are." The taxi pulled up in front of a small white stucco house that was in need of maintenance. The lawn looked like a threadbare blanket with patches of dirt showing through here and there. Isabel paid the driver over the seat and motioned to Grace to get out.

Jerry stood on the porch holding the door open as Grace helped Isabel up the steps. He was about Grace's age, and his face was sunburned from two days on the lake. Dusty brown hair stuck out in tufts from under his fishing hat decorated with lures and buttons. A cigarette hung from his lips.

"Oh, Jerry, I'm so glad you're here." Isabel didn't seem to notice that he didn't make a move to help her out of the car or up the steps.

"I just got home a couple of hours ago, but I figured you'd be home soon."

The smell of cigarette smoke was pungent and thick inside, reminding Grace of the casinos she had wandered in and out of the previous day. It seemed strange that he had been there long enough to smoke up the house and yet not come to the hospital to get his mother.

"This is Gloria. She's the one who called the ambulance." Grace extended her hand to Jerry, but he didn't shake it. He looked her up and down curiously.

Isabel inspected the living room and kitchen before she put her purse on the table and sat down heavily in the recliner. Dingy flow-ered wallpaper covered the walls giving Grace the idea that the home belonged to Isabel rather than Jerry.

"So…how did you get hooked up with Mom?" Jerry stubbed out his cigarette in an ashtray brimming with butts.

"She fell to the floor right in front of me."

"So you spent the night in the hospital with her?"

"Well, yes, I did." Grace tried to smile, but she had a feeling she was being interrogated.

"Do you often go stay all night in the hospital with strangers?"

Grace felt the dreaded heat drift up from the inner core of her body and perspiration form across her face.

"No, I was stranded by some friends…and…"

"And didn't have anything better to do?" he finished.

Grace was in a stranger's home and didn't want to argue, but she felt he was attacking her and she had to defend herself. Yet, she had told so many lies, she was beginning to confuse herself.

"Someone took my purse while I was helping your mother."

Jerry didn't hesitate. "So did you expect her to pay you for help-ing her?"

"I helped your mother because I wanted to. She begged me to go to the hospital with her." Grace's voice was elevating. "I'm here because she asked me to help her get home. If you want me to leave, I'll leave right now!" Grace grabbed her sunglasses, which was the only possession she had and moved toward the door.

"Take it easy. Don't get excited." Jerry took a deep breath. "Mom will be ticked off at me if I run you off. If she thinks you're okay, it'll have to be okay with me, I guess."

Grace, still distressed by the hot flash and upset by the confron-tation with Jerry, found herself fighting back tears. Suddenly, she felt totally exhausted.

"Would you mind if I just lie down on the sofa for a while? This whole ordeal has been more than I'm up to right now."

"This has been a tough day all around. I didn't catch a single fish all morning." Grace hoped he was joking, but he looked per-fectly serious.

"I know you must be worried about your mother. I'd really like to help out with her for a while…but if I don't get some sleep…" Tears trickled down her face, unheeded.

"Sure, we'll talk later." Jerry disappeared into the kitchen, but Grace knew he didn't really want her there.

Country western music blasted from the truck radio. Pete switched to another station to catch the news. The announcer was reporting on the bus wreck.

"Another passenger in the Baker bus accident has died today of complications, bringing the total to eleven. Two still remain in critical condition and one is missing. The missing woman is believed to be a teacher, Grace Partain of Highland. She's the wife of Philip Partain, owner of Partain Realtors located in the San Bernardino area. Searchers are continuing to look, but have not been successful in picking up Mrs. Partain's tracks."

"Well, can you beat that? Grace Partain. Who would have thunk it? Now what d'ya suppose happened to her?" LeRoy wondered out loud.

"If we could figure that out, it might be worth somethin'." The ash from Pete's cigarette flew away in the wind as he spoke.

"Like what?" LeRoy spat out the open window.

"Like…let's say we found her driver's license. What would that be worth?" Pete had an idea forming, but it was more fun to tease LeRoy a little before he gave it up.

"Ah…well, they might think it was a clue or somethin' and be glad to see it." LeRoy was having trouble following Pete's thinking.

"Yeah, but what if we found HER? What would that be worth?"

LeRoy's eyes widened. "I reckon we'd be heroes."

"Yeah…heroes. And how much do they pay heroes for finding someone?"

"They never said nothin' about no reward, but I bet we'd get our picture in the papers…and…our names on the radio."

"Yeah, but no money. How much do ya suppose they'd give us if we had her and we wanted to keep her?"

LeRoy was stuck. His face twisted into a curious squint. "What are you talkin' about, Pete? We don't have her!"

"No, but we know what she looks like. We know how tall she is and how much she weighs. We know her birthday and where she lives."

"Yeah, so what? I don't get what you're gettin' at."

Pete pulled the tow truck into the parking lot of the Wild Horse Casino and turned off the engine. He gazed off into space as if he were afraid if he focused on something it would interrupt his train of thought. He wiped the sweat off his brow and grinned at LeRoy.

"Let me see that license."

"What ya want it for?" LeRoy extracted the crumpled license with his greasy fingers and handed it over.

Pete studied the license for a moment. "I bet Mr. Partain is plenty worried about Gracie by now. He'd prob'ly do most anything to get her back. She's a mighty fine lookin' woman."

"So how the heck we gonna find her? I'm not goin' back out there and trudge around in the desert."

"No, stupid. Don't ya get it? We'll call Mr. Partain, tell him we've got Grace and ask for some money to return her." Pete had never come up with such a grandiose plan before. He was amazed at himself.

"We can't ask for very much 'cause we don't have her." LeRoy scratched his head. He really didn't get how this idea was going to work.

"Look, goofus! We'll call him and tell him we have Grace. We can even describe her. Then we'll tell him we'll give her back if he'll bring us $500,000. We'll get him to drop the money off someplace where we can get it and run."

"Hey, that sounds great. But how's he gonna get Grace back?"

"You are dumber than a box of rocks. We don't care if he ever gets her back, but we get the money and head to another state. We'll be rich!"

LeRoy understood that part and he began to take a liking to the whole idea.

"Okay, Pete. When are ya gonna call?"

"As soon as we git a cold drink." With a squeal of rusty door hinges, they jumped down from the truck and headed for the casino.

CHAPTER 4

Grace couldn't remember the exact moment she decided to become Gloria, but so far, things weren't going as she'd hoped. Jerry watched her every move and she wasn't certain of his intentions. If he was planning to make a move on her, she wasn't sure how she would handle it.

"How long are you planning on staying?" Jerry slid onto the sofa next to Grace.

"I...I...I'm between jobs, and I told you my purse was taken when I was trying to help your mother."

Jerry reached over and ran his fingers along the collar of Grace's shirt. "Were you thinking of asking my mom for money?"

"Of course not." Grace jumped up and headed for the kitchen. "I need a glass of water."

Jerry followed her. As she ran the water, he closed in behind her with his nicotine stained hands on the counter on both sides. She could smell his cigarette breath as his lips almost touched her neck.

"You could earn a little cash real quick if you wanted to."

Grace slid away from Jerry. She felt her anxiety grow and the cursed hot flash start deep inside, scattering her thoughts. *Not now. I've got to think straight and keep my wits about me.*

"What did you have in mind?" She tried to make her voice sound very businesslike and unseductive.

"I manage a little casino not far from here. How about doing some hostess work for a few days?"

"Hostess? What does that entail?"

"Easy. Just take cocktail orders and deliver drinks to patrons."

Grace had wanted adventure, but being a bar maid was quite a stretch from teaching school. She wasn't about to ask Jerry for money. Just the look in his eyes made her think he had other ideas. And after his earlier comments, she couldn't ask Isabel for cash. She had thought Isabel might offer her fare to return home, but that hadn't happened. Grace could have called at least three banks and twice as many friends who would have sent her the money in a heartbeat, but doing that would ruin her plan to just disappear. One phone call would make her presence known and she'd be right back in Highland living a lonely life with a husband who was never there and teaching children who were never hers.

"When do I start?"

If she was going to make the plan work, she had to take some risks. Earlier, she'd had to smash a vase in the living room to distract Jerry and Isabel away from the TV during the local news. As Jerry cleaned up the water, Isabel washed the blood from Grace's hand and looked for a Band-Aid.

"Oh, I'm so clumsy. I am sorry," Grace had apologized.

"It's okay...if you're okay," Isabel replied.

By the time the mess was cleaned up, the weather forecaster was turning the show over to the sports reporter.

Whew! That was a close one.

"Hello." Phil had been sitting by the phone for several hours and he grabbed it on the first ring.

"Mr. Partain?" Pete said, panting a bit from the struggle to get himself into the phone booth.

"Yes?"

"Ya wanna see your wife?" Pete blurted out.

"...uh...uh...who is this? Sgt. Childers?"

"No, it ain't Sgt. Childers. It's the guy who's got your little Gracie."

"Who is this?" Phil demanded.

"Wouldn't you like to know?" Pete left the phone booth door slightly ajar so he could get some air and so LeRoy could listen in. They grinned at one another.

"Let me speak to her, please," Phil was confused.

"Can't do that right now. I'll be needin' some money before I can let you speak to her."

"Money! Who is this? What are you talking about?"

Pete grinned at LeRoy and gave him the AOK signal with his thumb and forefinger together.

"We'll be keepin' Gracie safe for ya until ya come up with $500,000."

"Listen, whoever you are. Mrs. Partain was in an accident."

"Yeah, we know all about it. The bus flipped over."

"Where did you find her?"

"Never mind where we found her. But those blue eyes sure are beauts and all 135 pounds of her wishes she could be home for her birthday on June twenty-fifth."

Phil wanted to reach through the phone and grip the throat of whoever was on the other end of the line. He tried to control his words and emotions.

"Don't hurt Grace...please."

"Oh, I wouldn't want to hurt one of those pretty blonde hairs. So how about the money?" LeRoy impatiently tapped on the door.

"I don't have $500,000."

"How long will it take to get it?"

"One or two days. Let me talk to Grace…let me hear her voice."

"No way. You get the money together and we'll call you tomorrow night about ten with instructions. And don't be thinkin' about calling the police or you'll never see Grace alive again. You have one day. One day. Make it count!"

"Wait a minute! WAIT!"

Pete slammed the receiver down and slapped the phone with a gleeful yip.

"He went for it!"

"We're gonna be rich." LeRoy wiped the tobacco out of the corner of his mouth with his sleeve and tried to help Pete pry himself out of the phone booth.

***

Phil put down the receiver in disbelief. His emotions were running wild. That morning, he thought Grace might be dead in a bus wreck. Then he thought she might be alive, but lost on the desert somewhere. Now, she was alive but in the hands of a kidnapper. *How could this be?*

It was more than Phil could comprehend. He put his head in his hands and cried, something he had never done before. His shoulders shook and salty tears dripped on the front of his shirt.

Why did she go on this stupid trip anyway? WHY? She hates gambling. Why didn't I talk her out of it…or go with her. Oh, Grace, what have I done?

Dear Heavenly Father, please help me. I don't know what to do.

Phil hadn't prayed in years. He always thought he had his life under control. God, he thought, was for weak people who couldn't make it on their own. But today he was weak, and he needed help badly.

It was getting dark by the time Phil got up from the sofa. He didn't know where to start. Pacing from room to room, he finally stopped at the file cabinet and began to rifle through the information on their accounts. He could put his hands on $100,000 cash, but he wasn't sure he could do it in one day. He and Sheldon had invested in property, mutual funds, and stocks. Maybe between them, they could come up with the rest by selling their stocks. But how was he going to do it without drawing attention or telling someone what was going on? The last thing he wanted to do was endanger Grace's life.

Sergeant Childers ran in under the beating rotors of the helicopter. Dust whirled around him as he approached the pilot's open door.

"Well? Any sight of her?" he yelled at the top of his lungs.

"Nothing!" The pilot shrugged helplessly.

"What now?"

"It's your call. We've done a grid search for at least a five-mile radius. Unless there's a hole or a cave or something we can't see…it's pretty open and unprotected out there. We didn't see a sign of anything. How about the Jeeps? Did they see anything?"

Childers shook his head. "Nah, not so much as a footprint."

"So, what'll it be? Do we keep on or quit? It's getting dark, but we could try some infrared later and see if we see anything."

"No, I guess we'll quit for tonight. We've been searching for more than twelve hours. Call me tomorrow and let's see if anyone responds to seeing her picture on the news. Maybe we'll get a break."

Childers ducked away from the chopper. He knew it was time to go home, but he just couldn't leave this case alone. He was thirty-five years old and had dreamed of a more exciting brand of law enforcement. However, he'd found his niche in the Baker area and was respected by the citizenry. While he was only one of the thousand men employed by the San Bernardino Sheriff's Department, he was beginning to feel like an Andy Fife of Mayberry. This was the first case he'd had that was out of the ordinary and it was getting under his skin. Where had the woman disappeared to?

It doesn't make sense that her purse was on the bus and she wasn't. Maybe she wandered into the road during the storm and someone picked her up and gave her a ride. To where? Wouldn't she want her purse? Wouldn't she have called the police for her belongings? Maybe she had amnesia and someone on the highway picked her up and took her to the hospital. Surely someone in the hospital would have put two and two together when the other victims were brought in. What could have happened to Grace Partain?

Childers went home, but he continued to try to figure out what it was that he was missing…besides Grace Partain.

Grace was in a hurry to get out of Isabel's little house. Isabel was feeling the effects of the medication the doctor prescribed and slept most of the day. That suited Grace's plan just fine. She convinced Jerry to leave the TV off and keep the house quiet fearing they would televise her picture at least one more time before the story became old news.

Jerry, on the other hand, wanted to hover over Grace. Without the TV, there wasn't much to busy herself with except Isabel's Modern Maturity magazines or Jerry's Playboys. Neither appealed to her, so she settled down with a photo album from the coffee table.

"Mom said you're single, huh?"

"Divorced."

"Boyfriend?"

"No." She thought about saying yes just to discourage him. But she was afraid he would be wondering why she wasn't calling him to send her some money, or come and get her, or something.

"Date much?"

"No." Grace wished he'd just drop it. She was afraid to be rude or try to shut him down because she wasn't sure how he would react.

"Maybe we'll go to a show or something my next night off."

"I don't think I'll be here that long. I just need enough money to get some clothes and a ticket home."

She felt trapped. Funny, she would have loved it if Phil had been this attentive. He had everything she wanted, but was aloof and never shared much with her. She remembered how infatuated she was by his good looks and suave manner on their first date. They had driven up to Lake Arrowhead to Chandell's Restaurant. No one had ever treated her so special. The restaurant was a beautiful place with lovely sky blue linen napkins and matching tablecloths. Phil insisted the waitress bring Grace a twist of lemon for her water before he would order. Then he did all the ordering and made sure they had her favorite dessert, bread pudding, before he was satisfied everything was just right. When they arrived at her apartment, he left her sitting in the car. She thought he was going around to open the car door for her, so she waited. Several seconds elapsed before he came bounding over a nearby hedge, slung open the door, swept into a low bow, and with a big grin presented her with a lovely rose. They both laughed. Undoubtedly, a neighbor was short one beautiful rose the next morning. It had been many years since he'd made her feel special like that. And now, she was alone in a strange house with a creep that she had to depend on for her care.

Jerry gave her a couple of his old shirts. They were large, but he promised she'd have a uniform to wear at the casino. When he suggested she start work right away, it was almost a relief.

"Come on, Gloria. Let's get to the casino. You might as well get started."

Grace actually looked forward to being around people for a while. Anything seemed better than having Jerry constantly slobbering over her. Before leaving, she peeked in at Isabel, who was snoring away peacefully.

They arrived in the alley behind the casino and Jerry used his key to let them in the back door. He guided Grace to a small dressing room filled with cleaning products, mops, tools, and uniforms. He looked her over and selected a shirt and pants, handing them to her. He hesitated as though he were going to wait while she changed, but when Grace made no move, he left, closing the door behind him. There were several lockers, so she rolled up her own clothes and put them in one of the empties. A couple of the lockers had padlocks, but she wasn't storing any valuables. She had none.

In a few minutes, she emerged with a new look. Tight black jeans with a red satin shirt made up the uniform. It made her skin crawl to think she was wearing clothes someone else had worn before her. The white tennis shoes were her own. Thank goodness the children in her class couldn't see her. Thank goodness her friends couldn't see her. Thank goodness, this was only a temporary situation until she had enough cash to leave.

Grace still could not believe she was going through with this. But if she was going to get out of town without giving away her whereabouts, this was the only way. She had waited tables during college while Phil got started in business.

Jerry was all business as he gave Grace directions. "All you have to do is walk around, smile, offer free drinks, take orders, and deliver the drinks. There are three other girls, and each one covers a separate area. Check with them and see where they want you."

"Where are the *girls?*" Grace couldn't keep the sarcasm out of her voice as she looked around the seedy casino.

"Sadie is over by the bar. Lianne is up near the front door, and Madeline is back by the crap tables. Let's take a quick walk around and I'll introduce you."

Lianne & Sadie were in their early twenties. Lianne was working her way through college and Sadie had moved from Utah to be on her own. Madeline looked older than Grace and wasn't a bit friendly. She eyed Jerry as if to say, "So where did this one come from?"

Jerry tweaked Madeline's arm and she winced. Grace noticed and wondered if it was a show of affection, punishment, or reassurance that she was his favorite girl.

"If you have any problems, just let me know," Sadie giggled and batted her false eyelashes. Red curls pulled up in a ponytail added to her impish look. She was thick around the middle but not overweight. Grace didn't perceive Sadie as someone to go to with a problem. Abruptly, Madeline spoke directly to Grace.

"Just don't get in my territory. My tips are my tips," Madeline growled, making it clear that the high rollers at the crap table were hers.

"Okay, that's enough standing around. Let's get to work. Go get 'em, Gloria." Jerry handed Grace a tray and slapped her on the rear end.

Grace felt the slow burn start from within and burst out in drenching perspiration that soaked through parts of the satin blouse. She took a deep breath and tried to calm her raging anxiety. *Dear God, please don't let me flip my lid. Help me relax and get control.* She tried to make sense of what she was doing here, but nothing was making much sense right now. There was no plan from here. And here was pretty dismal.

"Hey, how 'bout a drink over here, babe?" a burly man with a frayed denim shirt and hairy arms shouted. He dug into a plastic bucket of silver tokens he was holding. Three empty cocktail glasses were lined up next to the slot machine he was playing.

Smile, offer free drinks, take orders, and deliver. Grace forced a smile, and reached down to clear the empties away.

"Little lady gonna clean house or get me a drink?" He touched the silky fabric of her blouse sleeve and let his hand slide up against her jaw line.

"What would you like? Compliments of the house." Grace turned just enough so the tray created a barrier between her and the man.

"Compliments of the house, huh? Make it whiskey…something real *smooooth*?" He dug in the pay tray for a coin and let a silver token slide down into her breast pocket.

The weight of the coin pressing against her made her feel as though he had reached inside her clothing to put it there. She felt queasy as she walked quickly toward the bar. The empty glasses shook against one another as a wave of revulsion washed over her. The tray nearly slipped from her hands as she sat it down on the bar. All three glasses toppled over noisily against the ashtray and two crashed to the floor.

As Grace reached for a towel to clean up the mess, she noticed a newspaper on the barstool next to her, and on the front page she saw her own face staring up at her. The caption read, "Highland School Teacher Disappears." She folded the paper, put it under her arm, and rushed toward the restroom.

CHAPTER 5

On his way to the Las Vegas hospital, Sergeant Childers could not get Grace off his mind. He felt somehow responsible for her disappearance. It had happened in his jurisdiction and he wasn't about to leave it unsolved.

Things were usually pretty quiet in Baker, but this case really had him stymied. It had started as a freak bus accident and now was turning into a real mystery. He was in a hurry to see if hospital personnel might remember Grace. A serious investigation called for more than pulling out a ticket book and writing a citation, and he didn't even do that very often.

He hadn't been in the Las Vegas Hospital since his visit with a cousin who had an emergency appendectomy. He'd had trouble getting anyone's attention when his cousin needed a bedpan. He should have worn his uniform, it might have gotten more cooperation.

In an hour, he managed to talk to most of the orderlies and nurses that were there on duty the night of the accident. Some thought the woman in the photograph he showed them looked vaguely familiar, but they couldn't remember when or where they'd seen her. She definitely had not been admitted as a patient.

The photo showed Grace in a dark St. John knit suit. Her eyes were slightly averted which made her look dignified and aloof.

Just as Sergeant Childers was about to give up, Dr. Dornan swept by.

"Excuse me, doctor. Were you in the ER the night of the bus wreck?"

"Yes, I was." The doctor looked at the sergeant suspiciously.

"Could you answer a few questions?" Childers began, hopefully.

"Are you from the press?" the doctor frowned.

Childers showed his identification and badge before he continued. He had forgotten he wasn't in uniform.

"No, I'm Sergeant Childers from the sheriff's department, and I'm investigating the disappearance of Grace Partain...the woman who disappeared from the bus the same night as the wreck."

He held out the photo to Dr. Dornan. Dornan looked closely at the image and said, "Yes, I remember seeing her photo on TV."

"Do you remember seeing her that night?"

"She looks familiar, but things were pretty crazy that night. Three critical on top of the usual crisis...overdoses, suicide, heart attacks...wait a minute, there was a woman who..."

Dornan rubbed his forehead as if to massage the memory back into his head.

"There was a woman brought in that night with a heart attack."

"Was it this woman?" Childers felt the energy growing in his chest. He held the photo up again.

"No...no. I'd have to check the records, but there was an older woman with...chest pains and this looks a lot like her daughter."

"Daughter?" That didn't make any sense. Childers didn't know where Grace's mother lived or if she was even living, but if she lived in or near Vegas, Mr. Partain would have mentioned it.

"Yes, do you want me to find her name?"

Childers stuck the photo back into his pocket. He felt like the air had been knocked out of him.

"Sure, that'd be fine, thanks." He didn't see how this could possibly be the lead he needed, but he didn't want to foolishly overlook a detail that might direct him to Grace.

"Say…how about that bus driver, Fulton? He made a statement about the dust storm, did they bring him in?"

"Yes, they did and he was conscious when I first saw him."

"Did he make it?" Childers's hopes rose again.

"He's alive, but he's in a coma."

"Shoot, that's too bad. If he comes around, could you call me at this number, please." He handed his card to Dr. Dornan.

Childers left the hospital with a name, number, and address. Isabel Hodges. He checked his watch. It was getting late and he needed to get back home to Baker. He had gone by his house after work just long enough to shower, change clothes, greet his wife and two sons, and head for Vegas. Now it was almost 10:00 p.m.

He stopped at the nearest phone booth. A quick call wouldn't hurt, but it was too late to go across town looking for the address. Chances were it wasn't going to pan out anyway. The phone rang four times before there was a sleepy answer.

"Hello, is this Mrs. Hodges?"

"Yes, it is," Isabel pulled the pillow up to support the phone.

"I'm sorry to wake you. This is Sergeant Childers from the San Bernardino County Sheriff's Department."

"Oh my, has something happened to Jerry?" Waking from a sound sleep, she was shocked and confused.

"No, ma'am. Who's Jerry?"

Isabel had been sleeping most of the day. The medication made it difficult to focus.

"He's my son, but I think he's at work now. Tell me again, nothing has happened to him, has it?"

Childers could hear the concern in her voice and felt bad for calling so late.

"Listen, I'm sorry I bothered you. Could I speak to your daughter?"

"I don't have a daughter, Sergeant. Just Jerry, and he's at work." Before he could inquire further, she hung up the phone.

Grace fled to the woman's restroom, choking back tears as she stuffed the newspaper deep into the trash can. Whether it was the groping hands of the customer, the swat on the rear from Jerry, the broken glasses, or the queasy feeling in her stomach, she wasn't sure of what upset her the most. *I can't do it. What good can come of this? I feel so dirty. I've lied, changed my name, hidden from my husband and friends. What will happen to me? Someone is going to recognize me unless I can destroy every newspaper in Las Vegas.*

Like the rest of the dingy casino, the restroom was grimy and smelled of smoke. Dirty words were scratched into the paint and scraps of toilet paper cluttered the floor.

Grace entered the nearest stall and latched the door. A booklet sitting on the toilet paper dispenser caught her eye. It was titled *The Romans' Map to Heaven* and it had a question on the front. "If you died tonight, do you know if you would go to heaven?"

Grace could not hold back the flood of tears. *Oh, God, I don't know where I'm going tonight. Help me.*

"Gloria? " Not wanting to be found, Gloria held perfectly still with a wad of toilet paper over her nose.

"Gloria? Are you in here?" It sounded like Sadie.

"Sadie?" Gloria almost whispered.

"Gloria? Are you okay?" Sadie entered the restroom and tapped on the stall door.

Grace opened the door and fell into Sadie's arms in tears.

Phil had intended to stay home all day waiting for Sergeant Childers's call telling him Grace had been found. Better yet, he wished she'd come walking through the door and he'd wake up from this terrible dream. But the call from the kidnapper had totally shattered his already crumbling world and he could hardly think. Deciding whether to include Sheldon or not was another struggle.

"Sheldon, I need your help. Could you come to the house right away?"

"Sure, Phil. What's up? Have they found Grace?"

"Just come over, okay?" Phil hung up. He didn't want Sheldon to say something in the office that would raise suspicion.

Within a few minutes, Sheldon let himself in. All the way there, he had wondered how bad the news was. If they had found Grace, Phil would have said so right away. This had to mean very bad news. He found Phil pacing the living room.

Gesturing to the sofa, Phil said, "Sit down. I'm not even sure what I should tell you, but I don't know what to do."

Phil, who was used to donning a suit each day, had been uncertain of how to dress in a situation like this. The collar of his white shirt was unbuttoned and his tie lay across the back of the sofa. His hair was disheveled and his eyes were red. He wrung his hands and paced slowly back and forth, unable to stay still.

"Okay. So what's the word?" Sheldon could see Phil's distress, but his hesitation wasn't making it any easier.

"I got a call today from a guy who says he has Grace. And he wants five hundred thousand dollars in exchange for her safe return."

"What guy?" Sheldon's eyes widened. "I don't get it."

"A guy who sounds like a jerk says he has her and is holding her for ransom."

"Kidnapped? Grace was kidnapped? How could that happen?"

"All I know is he has her, he described her perfectly, and he's going to call back at five o'clock to tell me where to take the money. What am I going to do?"

"Did you tell the police?" Sheldon asked.

"No, I can't. He said he'd kill her if I told the police. He has the winning card and I have nothing." Phil started to cry. "I can't believe I let her go off by herself without even batting an eye. What was I thinking? It was stupid of me to let her go alone in the first place."

Sheldon had his own problems. He had a wife who didn't want him and wouldn't give five cents to have him back, and here was Phil with a wife he loved and would pay five hundred thousand dollars to get her home safely. At least some stranger wasn't holding Marilyn hostage.

"How much do you have in savings?" Seeing Phil cry rattled Sheldon. They were businessmen and they needed to get to work on some sort of plan. He could deal with planning better than he could with runaway emotions.

Phil wiped his nose with a tissue. "I have about $100,000, but I can't imagine walking into the bank and demanding to have it all without raising some suspicion."

"Between us, we've got lots of property and investments. With the two of us together, we'll just act like we've got some business deal going. Shoot, we've done business with Highland American Trust for years."

Phil settled down, relieved that they had a course of action. Leaving the house, he asked Sheldon to drive. Thoughts of Grace brought frightening pictures he couldn't put aside. *What was she going through right now? Had she suffered some injury in the accident that might not have been cared for? Did the animal who's holding her have her bound and gagged?* He tried to push away the images of Grace being touched or tormented. Was money the only motivation? Phil was afraid to say those thoughts aloud even to Sheldon.

In all their years as friends, Phil and Sheldon had shared almost everything, but nothing like this. Power-packed memories included high fiving one another during their high school football games when Phil was quarterback and Sheldon was the running back. Their senior year was a barrage of awards, banquets, newspaper pictures, and media coverage while the football team went undefeated. The two of them loved the spotlight and received scholarship offers from several colleges, but both elected to go into the real estate business and skip college.

Their plan to succeed in home sales had worked well. Nothing had really ever stood in their way. Any display of emotion had always been limited to wild elation over each closed sale or great golf game.

Sheldon's parents had retired in Florida and enjoyed good health and relaxing in the southern sunshine daily. Phil's parents had died in a car accident when he was just a baby. A loving grandmother had raised him, attending every one of those football games. Out on the field, he could hear her yelling at the top of her lungs. However, two days after graduation, he found her dead in her bed. The peaceful look on her face gave him a feeling that she didn't suffer and was now in a better place. Where? He wasn't sure, but he felt no need to anguish over this grandmother who always treated him right, lived happily, and died peacefully. The only tears he shed were at her bedside that day, and then he moved on to the world of real estate.

Success was Phil's goal. It was the mortar that made him. His constant achievements were the bricks that built his fortress. Unfortunately, he had walled out the one person who loved him, Grace. He thought she'd always be there, but seldom included her in the things he was doing. The two of them had begun to lead separate lives, he could see that now.

Nothing had ever hurt like this. To know that someone was holding Grace against her will...he didn't know where...who...or how…but he was going to get her back. He was going to do whatever was necessary to bring her home safely.

It was late afternoon when the two men finished their transactions. They had been creative and used their investments as collateral for a four hundred thousand dollar loan, and when they finished, they had a briefcase with the full amount in cash. Everyone in the business community knew they owned plenty of real estate and were good for the money. It was actually easier than either of them had expected.

"Hello, I need to talk to someone who's investigating the bus wreck that happened a couple of nights ago in Baker." The female voice was almost a whisper.

"This is deputy Holt. Sergeant Childers is the one you want to speak to, but he had to go into Vegas tonight." Holt tipped back in his swivel chair casually.

"Uh…can I leave a message?"

"Sure, no problem. First, could I have your name?" He slid the notepad into place and poised to take notes.

"I just want to tell you that Mr. Partain, the husband of Grace Partain, the missing woman, took five hundred thousand dollars in cash out of the bank today."

"You mean he robbed a bank?" Holt rocked forward and let the swivel chair squeak back to level with a jolt.

"No. He cashed out his savings and took out a loan. Maybe it's nothing, but it seemed strange to me."

"Whew! Okay, I need your name so we can get back to you."

Suddenly, the connection was broken and there was nothing but a dial tone.

Sadie gave Grace a squeeze. "Hey, what's the matter, Gloria?"

Grace left the bathroom stall and leaned against the sink. A quick glance in the mirror shocked her.

"Look at me. I'm a mess!"

"Did Jerry say something to you?" Sadie wetted a paper towel and blotted Grace's cheeks.

"No, I…it's just that…this is new to me and…" Grace realized Sadie could have been the age of her daughter if she'd had a daughter. And yet, Sadie seemed so mature and calm.

"You'll get the hang of it."

"Did you see? I broke two glasses." Grace took the paper towel from Sadie and patted it across the back of her neck.

"That's no big deal. We break glasses by the truckload around here. They're cheap and nobody cares as long as you keep taking orders and delivering drinks."

"Some guy touched me and I got upset." Grace shuddered as she remembered the coin. She pulled the silver token out of her blouse pocket.

"Ooh, and you got a dollar for it? Must have been worth it to someone!" Sadie laughed and made Grace chuckle through the tears. "I'm only kidding. Try to stay away from the jerks and ignore the hustlers. And get the bouncer if anybody gets too hard to handle. It's never easy because you have to serve them all. You'll learn as you go along."

"Thanks, Sadie. You're a lifesaver." Grace was determined to do the job now. "If I have any problems, I'll just tell Jerry."

"No!" Sadie almost shouted. "Don't do that! He'll make you pay in some other way."

Sadie didn't offer anything more, but Grace knew immediately she was right about Jerry. He was dangerous.

Pete slapped LeRoy on the back. Their celebration had started at State Line and continued all the way back to Barstow. They settled in at Buford's Bar and drank until the lights were shut off and the owner kicked them out. They supported one another as they staggered out to the tow truck.

"I'll drop you off," Pete slurred as he loaded LeRoy.

"We gonna work tomorrow?" The door squealed as it slammed shut and there was a long wait while Pete made his way around to the driver's side.

Pete was out of breath by the time he lifted himself into the seat. "We won't ever have to work again. All's we have to do tomorrow is make that phone call."

CHAPTER 6

Marilyn had finally called and asked Sheldon to come home. He was not about to pass up a chance to move back. It could mean Marilyn was ready to mend their relationship.

There wasn't much he could do for Phil right now except sit and wait for the phone to ring since he was dead set against calling in law enforcement. Sheldon knew the number of his father's friend in Las Vegas who was a private eye. Phil insisted they shouldn't call anyone, but Sheldon gave him the phone number anyway.

As Sheldon mounted the steps, he saw Marilyn peek out the side window. He hoped that was a good sign. It felt funny to knock at the door of his own home, but that seemed the safest plan for now. Marilyn waited a few moments to open the door as if she'd been pre-occupied in some other part of the house.

"Oh, it's you," she said rather flatly. She stood aside for Sheldon to enter.

"I was hoping for a warmer welcome," Sheldon walked to the desk and started sorting through a large pile of mail. "Anything important come?"

"Sheldon, could you just leave the mail for now? We need to talk."

"Okay." He backed away from the desk and followed her to the dining room table. "What do you want to talk about?"

"I want a divorce."

"Please don't do this, Marilyn. This is not a good time for me."

"A good time for you?! I'm the one who has been constantly alone. I'm the one who sits by while you chase after the almighty dollar." Marilyn's voice was rising to a shriek.

"Listen, please, Marilyn. Let's not do this right now, I can't think about this." Sheldon was overcome by the shock of Marilyn asking for a divorce on top of Grace's kidnapping and ransom. How could he tell her that he and Phil had just taken out a half a million dollars to save Grace? And Phil had asked to keep the whole thing quiet until Grace was safe at home, so he couldn't say anything without jeopardizing Grace's life.

"Well, excuse me, but unless you can come up with a better idea, I'm having divorce papers drawn up tomorrow."

"Marilyn, please…give me time to help Phil deal with Grace's disappearance. Then we'll talk about it."

"Grace probably got fed up and walked out across the desert. The vultures would give her more attention than Phil ever did!" She was nearly screaming.

Pete and LeRoy didn't meet up until mid-afternoon. By then, the temperature was well over one hundred degrees outside and Buford's was a cool place to nurse a hangover. Locals drifted in and out all day, catching up on the news and sipping down cold drinks.

"Hey, Pete. LeRoy. How you guys been?" They were regulars and every one knew them.

"Pool anyone?" LeRoy had a real knack for pool. As he played, he drank, and the more he drank, the more he talked.

"Me 'n Pete. We won't be driving that broken down ol' tow truck after tomorrow."

"Yeah?" replied his pool opponent. "What you gonna be drivin'?"

"Could be Porsche or a…"

Pete had less to drink than LeRoy and was listening to the conversation. He got up from the bar stool, grabbed LeRoy's baseball cap and thwacked him across the back of the head with it. "LeRoy's just dreamin'. Ain't ya, LeRoy?"

LeRoy dropped his pool cue and protected his head with his arms. "What d'ya do that fer, Pete? I didn't say nothin' about the mon…"

Pete rapped him again, harder. "Shut up, LeRoy before I have to shut you up!"

LeRoy muttered as he picked up the cue stick and continued the game. As the day wore on and they continued drinking, Pete got more and more edgy. Each time LeRoy started to talk about money, Pete got a little rougher in his efforts to keep LeRoy from talking too much. Pete didn't have a clear plan for getting the money from Phil Partain without getting caught. He knew that talking it over with LeRoy was a waste of time because besides being stupid, LeRoy was now very drunk. Pete knew whatever happened, it would be up to him to figure things out.

"I'm runnin' outa smokes. I'll be right back," Pete said as he staggered toward the door. LeRoy downed his drink and headed for the restroom.

Pete made his way slowly across the dimly lit parking lot. He opened the driver's door of the truck and reached under the seat for the last pack of cigarettes in the now empty carton. His rummaging covered the sound of footsteps behind him. Suddenly, something heavy thudded against his skull. He grabbed for the steering wheel as he went down, seeing stars and the blinking neon lights, but his fingers slipped away empty, and everything went dark.

By ten, Phil was pacing frantically from the den to the dining room and back. Every time the phone rang, he snatched it up quickly. First, it was Sheldon calling to see if the kidnapper had called yet.

"Don't tie up the line, Shel. I'll call you when I know something." Abruptly, he cut the connection.

Next, was Fran. "Phil, I nearly died when I saw Grace's picture on TV. Have you heard anything?"

"No, Fran, but thanks for calling." He tried to end it quickly.

"Is there anything I can do? You know Janine and Carol are also asking."

"No, Fran, but thanks for calling." He tried again to end the call.

"Listen, Phil, I'm sure they'll find her."

"Thanks, Fran. I hope so." That was it. He hung up without saying goodbye.

There was another ring. Phil wished he could let the answering machine pick it up, but he was afraid it would be the kidnapper and he'd hang up. So he answered.

"Frank Wilburn here."

"Yes, Frank?" Phil had opened escrow on the ten million dollar complex Wilburn purchased through Partain Realtors on the day Grace left for Vegas. He was glad to have wrapped it up so smoothly.

"Sorry to hear about your wife. Have you heard anything yet?"

"No, but thanks for asking. It's good to hear from you." He was surprised that Wilburn called so late.

"You may not think so. It seems we've hit a bit of a snag."

Now was no time to cut him short. Frank Wilburn was a big investor and Phil did not want to lose the account.

"A bit of a snag? How's that?"

"I think...that is...my partners think...can we just say that we'd like to back off."

"Back off?" This was a million dollar commission, Phil's biggest ever. He tried to keep calm, but his heart was pounding.

"Look, Phil. Let's get together tomorrow and talk about it. There are a couple of new issues we need to discuss."

Phil would be on the road to get Grace by tomorrow. There was no way he could promise to meet with Wilburn. "I can't do that, Frank."

"You can't do what? Meet with me?" Now Wilburn sounded a little put off.

"No, I've got something I have to do tomorrow." There was a pause. Wilburn wasn't accustomed to being refused. Everyone always jumped to do whatever he needed because of the money and power he wielded.

"I think we need to put a stop to the escrow." It sounded like a threat to Phil.

"Listen, Frank. I don't know what the problem is. I thought you were happy with the deal as it stood." Phil switched the receiver to the other ear so he could wipe his sweaty palm on his slacks.

"You stop by my office tomorrow," Frank persisted.

"No, Frank. Not tomorrow!" Grace was the most important thing now. Forget the million dollars, forget Wilburn. Phil just wanted to get her home and time was precious.

"Okay, Phil. Maybe I can call Hargrave."

"Fine. Call Sheldon."

End of conversation. Phil knew he had alienated Wilburn, but he didn't care anymore. He just cared about getting Grace home again safely.

He slumped into the leather rocker and looked around him. In his den, surrounded by trophies and awards, he realized he had lost the one thing that was priceless to him. He picked up a framed picture from the table beside him. It showed him receiving a sales award with Grace by his side. She was always supportive, she was always there for him, she was always by his side. He realized he had really never taken an interest in anything she did. Bridge wasn't his cup of tea. Only once in nineteen years did he attend any of Grace's school functions. It was a Christmas pageant she directed.

He recalled that Grace had been at school all day, making last minute set changes and stitching up costumes. When Phil arrived, the program was just about to begin. He sat on the left aisle about half way back. He saw Grace adjusting robes and halos as children entered through the side door. Unlike her usual look of perfection, a strand of hair hung limply in the middle of her forehead and Phil marveled at how cute she looked. She'd been working on the program for weeks coordinating kids, parents, musicians, actors, sets, and costumes.

The program was a smashing success. They had honored the Christian customs as well as Kwanza and Channukah, and ended with a rousing chorus of Feliz Navidad. Phil searched for Grace as the crowd cheered for her to come forth. Pushing the twist of hair up away with one hand, she brushed tears of joy and exhaustion from her cheeks.

Phil remembered how proud he was of her at that moment, and he felt the tear slide down on his own cheek now.

The phone rang again at eleven. It was Sheldon. "Phil, what the heck are you thinking? Wilburn said you refused to meet with him tomorrow and he's got some concerns to discuss."

"Yeah well, I have concerns, too. Right now all I can think of is having Grace back home safely."

"Have you heard anything yet?"

"No, and until I do, I'm going to stay right by the phone."

Sheldon sighed loudly. "So what if we lose the Wilburn deal?"

"Life goes on. And I want my life to go on with Grace. I've been putting business first for too long."

"You're beginning to sound like Marilyn. She's threatened me with divorce papers."

"So what are you going to do?"

"I wish I knew. I couldn't tell her about the ransom and the money we pulled out..." Sheldon felt his emotions rising so he cut the conversation short. "We'll talk tomorrow. I'll call you before I go to the office."

Again Phil waited...and waited...and waited.

After their conversation in the restroom, Grace gathered up her courage and worked steadily all night, taking orders and serving drinks. There was constant activity and the time went quickly. Although some customers sat for hours as though they had been painted in their positions, the constant jingling of bells and clattering of money gave the illusion of action.

The casino was rather shabby, but the clientele varied from unshaven seedy looking characters to well-dressed patrons who seemed to be glad to be away from the maddening crowd. Grace noticed the contrast.

"Excuse me, may I trouble you for a soda water with a twist of lime?" The voice came from a handsomely dressed man at the craps table, and Grace responded with a smile. When she returned with his drink he placed a two-dollar tip on her tray, and she noticed his gold Rolex, just like Phil's, with diamonds on each number. A knot formed in her stomach as she thought about the impact her disappearance might have on Phil. So far, she was worse off than before. This was certainly no wonderland.

By 5:00 a.m. her legs throbbed and her feet hurt. Her wrist was cramped from carrying the tray and her pockets were full of silver tokens. Jerry had told her they would leave by six. She wished Sadie would invite her to stay at her apartment, but somehow she felt indebted to Jerry and Isabel for the job. What would he do if she alienated him? Sadie had warned her not to cross him.

"Come on, Gloria. Let's get out of here and get some shut-eye." Jerry reached around her waist and untied her apron. She already dreaded returning to the house with him. Sadie and Lianne said goodnight and stayed behind to finish their shift. Madeline watched Jerry escort Grace out the back door and then headed for the storage room.

It felt weird to be going back to a strange house with a man she couldn't trust. His loyalty to his mother didn't even seem admirable.

The sun was beginning to come up and all Grace wanted to do was get some sleep. *Oh Lord, please let me rest in peace.* If Jerry made any advances, he would have a fight on his hands.

There was no fight. They arrived at the house without a word. As Grace got out of the car, she saw the morning newspaper on the walk. Seeing her photo center front, she scooped it up and tucked it vertically between her arm and body, hoping Jerry wouldn't notice. He didn't. He ushered her into a small extra bedroom and sauntered off without so much as a goodnight. Good. That was just what she'd prayed for. She sneaked into the bathroom for a shower. It had been two days of spit baths, and Grace basked in the lukewarm spray. Isabel had left make-up, powder, shampoo, comb, and a few things out where Grace could use them.

As she was drying off, she heard Isabel and Jerry conversing in the adjacent bedroom. Quickly and quietly, she put on the oversized T-shirt Jerry had loaned her and stepped into the hall. It seemed Isabel was agitated about a phone call. Had someone called? Grace could only catch bits and pieces, nothing was clear. She wondered if Isabel had seen her picture on TV and called someone, but she was too desperate for sleep to think of what to do next. So far, she had just let things happen as they would. Tonight, all she wanted was sleep…with the newspaper stuffed between the mattresses. As she drifted off, she asked herself the question, "If I died tonight, where would I go?"

CHAPTER 7

The sun began to sneak in between the vertical blinds of the hospital room. LeRoy was asleep in the chair. Pete's rotund form filled the bed. A white bandage covered his head and his eyes were dark caves with blackened circles like hammocks under them. The white sheets and blankets presented a striking contrast to the figure whose grease and grime had defied the soapy sponges of the nursing aides.

"Time for breakfast. Anyone hungry?" The day nurse pulled cords, opening the blinds and flooding the room with light.

Both LeRoy and Pete stirred. "Oh. Ouch. Oh. Who hit me?" Pete's hand touched the bandages on his head gingerly. "*Oooh.* What hit me? Where am I?"

"Barstow Hospital," replied the nurse a little too cheerfully.

LeRoy dodged the orderly who delivered the food tray and went to the other side of the bed. He took a pinch of snuff from the can in his hip pocket and stuck it in his bottom lip, warming up to tell what had happened the night before.

But Pete got the jump on him. "You sorry sucker, you were gonna make the call and get the money without me, weren't ya?"

"I swear, Pete, I didn't hit you." He'd thought of it often enough, but Pete outweighed him by eighty pounds and had always been his defender against others. "Besides, I don't even know the phone number."

It didn't take much thought for Pete to realize LeRoy wasn't smart enough to devise his own plan and was probably too chicken to hit him.

"Maybe someone in the bar just got sick of seein' you pick on me, slappin' me in the head with my hat and tellin' me to shut up about the money all the time."

Pete speculated for a moment. "Or maybe somebody thought we had some money already, figured I would have it on me, and wanted to steal it." He had been drinking coffee as he talked. LeRoy helped himself to a piece of the dry toast. Suddenly, Pete put the coffee cup down with such force it slopped over into the oatmeal. "The money! We never called Partain! Give me the phone!" The quick movement made his head throb, and he thought of a way to stall Partain until he could get out of the hospital.

A good night's sleep helped Sergeant Childers make some calculated decisions. He called off the Jeep and helicopter searchers. With nothing more than sagebrush to hide under, he felt sure Grace Partain wasn't out there. The Hodges' lead from Dr. Dornan hadn't panned out, but there was still the bus driver.

Entering the station, he saw the message on the desk. "Partain took a half-million dollars out of his accounts yesterday." Immediately, he tried to imagine why Partain would be getting together such a large sum of money now. If he was going to kill his wife, he wouldn't plan a bus accident that would kill eleven other people and might leave her alive. If he was planning on leaving her, why would he do it when she was already missing? That didn't make sense. If she were dead, he would get all the money anyway. If he was worried about her disappearance, why would he be making any financial decisions?

He had seemed genuinely worried. He dialed the Partain home in Highland, but the line was busy.

Phil heard the call waiting signal, but he was not about to interrupt this call.

"You bring the money to the Full House Casino on Chandler Street at ten o'clock tomorrow night," Pete demanded.

"Tomorrow night? Why not tonight?" Phil was eager to get this over with.

"Can't today. Tomorrow night in the alley by the backdoor."

"Let me talk to Grace then."

"Not today. Tomorrow night when we have the money."

Phil gritted his teeth and hissed, "That's almost two days away! I have to know that Grace is all right."

A female orderly entered to take Pete's breakfast tray away. He covered the mouthpiece and asked her how she was doing. "I'm just fine," she replied softly as he uncovered the mouthpiece.

Phil thought he heard a woman's voice. "Was that Grace?"

"Yep, and she's doin' just fine. You heard all you're gonna hear. I'll see ya tomorrow night." The call was disconnected.

Phil ran his hands through his uncombed hair and made a growling sort of sound that a bear might make if it's cub was lost. What was he going to do for two days? He called Sheldon at the office.

Their normal conversation about business was set aside. Phil told Sheldon about the phone call and the plan to make the exchange on Tuesday night. His voice was shaking.

"What will I do today and tomorrow? I'll go nuts!"

"You could meet Wilburn with me." Sheldon reverted to their usual solution for everything, work.

"Forget it. I can't think about work now."

"Did you get any sleep?"

"Very little, but all I can think of is what that creep might be doing to Grace."

"Hey, let's not talk about that. There isn't anything you can do."

"That's the worst part of it." Phil was on the brink of tears again.

"Listen, buddy, try to get some sleep today, and I'll take care of Wilburn."

"I already made him mad, but I just couldn't deal with it then." Both men were stuck in similar, but different situations, and were worried, exasperated, and stressed. They agreed to talk later.

Phil felt paralyzed. He couldn't just go about his life for two days pretending nothing was happening. Maybe a drive would do him good. Digging in his pocket for the keys, he found the scrap of paper Sheldon had given him with the number of the private investigator.

Phil called the number. When Ralph Moore answered, Phil didn't know how to start. He was hesitant to talk about Grace and the bus accident, but there was no other way.

"Yes, I did see that on the news last night," said Ralph. "I think they even ran her picture. So what's the deal?"

Phil told him about the phone call, the money, and the plan to meet.

"What do I do now? I can't go to the police. The kidnapper would kill her." His frantic voice sounded like a helpless child. Phil wasn't thinking rationally anymore.

Ralph asked questions to see what information he had to work with. There wasn't much. All Phil could be sure of was there was at least one man and they would be meeting at the Full House Casino in Las Vegas on Tuesday night at ten. He told about hearing a woman's voice and hoping it meant Grace was okay.

"I'm not sure what I can do." Ralph quoted his fee, they exchanged phone numbers, and agreed to keep in touch if anything happened on either end. Meanwhile, Ralph promised to do what he could with what little information he had.

There wasn't much to go on, but Phil tried to fan that flicker of hope into a warming fire. *Lord, forgive me for waiting until now to seek you. You've been faithful to me when I have been unfaithful to you. Please keep Grace safe, guide Mr. Moore, and help me to keep my wits about me.* An unexpected peacefulness brought a deep relaxing sleep that lasted most of the day.

The ringing phone woke him. It was Marilyn. They exchanged pleasantries.

"Phil, what's going on?"

"What do you mean?" Phil rubbed his eyes.

"Number one, have you heard anything about Grace?"

"No, I haven't."

"You sounded like you were sleeping."

"I was. I didn't sleep last night and I'm exhausted."

Marilyn continued, "Number two, I saw an attorney about drawing up divorce papers today."

"I'm sorry to hear that. You both...well, I wish you would try to work it out."

"I can't work it out by myself and the only thing that interests Sheldon is working on the next property deal."

"What can I do?" Phil was sure there was more coming. Marilyn was so full of her own problems she wasn't even thinking about what Phil was going through the past two days.

"Well...I went to the bank today to check out our finances so I'd know what was available. They told me you and Shel have most of our investments tied up right now. How could that happen without me knowing about it? What's going on?"

Phil was stuck. Telling Marilyn about the kidnapper wasn't part of the plan. He'd already alienated Fran, Mr. Wilburn, and probably Sheldon.

"We had to get a large sum of money right away."

"Large sum of MY money is what you mean. When that attorney figures out our assets, those investments had better show up. I stood by Sheldon all these years, and I'm going to get what's coming to me." Her anger was rising and her accusations more pointed. "Do you hear me, Phil?"

"Yes, I hear." His answer was empty.

"I don't know what the two of you are up to, but I want that money now!" she demanded loudly.

"We had to get some cash to help Grace..."

"Oh, don't tell me, let me guess. I suppose you've decided to play the doting husband and offer a big fat reward to the person who finds her."

Marilyn had always been the most emotional one of the foursome. Usually, she flew into a rage that dissipated quickly. But she had never threatened divorce. Phil realized that Grace hadn't either, but lately she had been completely closed to him, even before and after their rare intimacies. He had put work ahead of her for so long that he had shoved her completely out of his grasp. If he could just hold her again and ask for another chance. Everything was falling apart at once and for the first time in his life, he had no control.

"Marilyn, would it make any difference if I told you I needed the money to get Grace back safely?"

"Get Grace...I don't understand. I thought she was missing." Marilyn's voice became quiet and thoughtful.

"I thought she was, too, until a guy called and asked for five hundred thousand dollars in ransom money."

"Oh, my god! Someone has her?! Oh, my god! I am so sorry, Phil!"

He wondered about her sincerity. Sheldon had been his best friend since high school, but Marilyn was another matter. She resented Phil for all the time he spent with Sheldon and she was jealous of Grace's education and beauty. In the early years, the two couples had attended numerous events together, but the two women had little in common. Marilyn was more at ease with her fellow beauticians while Grace was often busy correcting papers or enjoying a quiet bridge game with teacher friends. Both Partains tried to steer clear of Marilyn's snide remarks and displays of anger whenever things didn't go her way.

"Thanks, Marilyn. Hopefully this will be over tomorrow and Grace will be home and safe."

"What about the...the money? How will we recoup a half a million dollars?"

As Phil expected, it was the money that concerned Marilyn most.

It was mid-afternoon when Grace woke to the sound of the TV blasting. Stretching and flexing, she felt stiff and sore. She was not eager to face Jerry and Isabel. It would be hours before she and Jerry returned to the casino, and without wheels, she was trapped there. Maybe she could take a walk and buy some necessities with her tips. She swung her legs over the edge of the bed and was hit by a sudden wave of dizziness. Steadying herself, she realized she hadn't had a full meal in three days, just a snack here and there.

Breakfast would be the first order of business. She dressed in one of Jerry's old shirts and the black jeans. She sparingly used the make-up items Isabel had offered and joined Jerry in the kitchen.

"Coffee, Gloria?" Jerry offered.

"Sure, thanks." Grace sat at the table and remembered why there was no morning paper and that she had forgotten to even read it.

"I'd offer you the paper, but the stupid delivery guy must have missed our house this morning. I couldn't find it anywhere."

"Oh well, no news is good news, they say," Grace faked a light chuckle.

Grace was starved and didn't know how to go about requesting breakfast in the home of these strangers. She had at least thirty dollars in tips. If Jerry didn't offer food soon, she could walk somewhere and grab a bite, but it was already over one hundred degrees outside and she didn't want to go far. "I think I could treat us all to breakfast somewhere, if you think your mother is up to it."

"I won't hear of it. We'll eat right here." Isabel entered the kitchen and set to work frying sausage and eggs. Grace pitched in and put the bread in the toaster as Jerry drank a cup of coffee, smoked a cigarette, and gazed at the small TV on the counter.

Grace was thankful for Isabel's offer. She could hardly wait to sit down and eat. The coffee had hit hard with nothing to coat her empty stomach. Her first bite was tasty and satisfying. Savoring every morsel, Grace felt like someone who had been shipwrecked without food. Then a sudden wave of nausea caused her to put the fork down and sit back in the chair. After a few moments, she gingerly took another bite of toast and a sip of coffee. Her stomach felt as if she had been on a roller coaster. Bite by bite, she nursed down each swallow and waited. Finally, with some egg and sausage still on her plate, she finished the toast, thanked Isabel for the meal, and headed back to the bedroom to lie down.

Perspiration beaded on Grace's brow and she prayed for the calm to come. Thirty minutes later, she felt relaxed and fine. She assumed the brief discomfort was from eating the fried food after not having a decent meal in days. People her age sometimes had to watch what they ate. Better lay off the sausage. She'd have to be more careful and make sure she ate before they went back to the casino for the night.

Grace hadn't even looked at the newspaper she had hidden under the mattress. She took it out and read more about the search being called off. The bus driver was still in a coma and the remaining injured passenger was making a rapid recovery. The article stated that the missing passenger—Grace—was a mystery and was being investigated by the sheriff's department in Baker. She tore off the column, folded it in half, and put it in her jeans pocket. Then she returned the paper to its hiding place.

In the early evening, Jerry thumped on her bedroom door and entered almost before she answered. "Want to take a little ride?"

"That would be great. I need to pick up a few things…toiletries for sure. Maybe I'll have enough tips tomorrow to buy an outfit of new clothes."

"Maybe you can pay your way around here if you're going to stay." Jerry scowled and Grace felt like a child who had just been scolded for taking something that didn't belong to her.

"I didn't expect to stay here for free, but I…well, I thought… maybe in a few days…" Grace was at a loss. She was afraid to stay and afraid to leave. "I really can't pay you anything until I get a paycheck."

Jerry reached down and jerked Grace to her feet. "You can pay me on the installment plan." He clumsily tried to kiss her on the neck, but Grace twisted away.

"Jerry, please don't do that. Give me a few days."

"A few days to do what, honey…warm up?"

"A few days to earn some money, so I can pay my room and board. Nothing else." She wanted to make her intentions clear to him.

"Nothing else, huh? We'll see." He left the room, but Grace knew it wasn't over.

Pete held an ice pack on his swollen head. The doctor had refused to discharge him even though the nurses were all hoping for his departure. LeRoy had spent the morning flipping channels with the remote control and spitting tobacco juice in the trash can while

Pete buzzed the nurses with requests for juice, coffee, an extra pillow for LeRoy, and more green Jell-O. Whenever a nurse or doctor entered the room, Pete moaned and rolled his eyes back in his head.

"Mr. Jensen, I know you're eager to get out of here, but there are signs of a fairly serious concussion, and I'd feel safer if we kept you until tomorrow morning."

"Oh dang, Pete. Am I gonna hafta sleep sittin' up in this chair again tonight?"

"Shut your whinin,' LeRoy! I'm the one who got my head beat in. I'm the one with the percussion." Pete sighed and sheepishly turned to the doctor who was trying to stifle a smile. "I guess if I have to stay, I'll stay." And he pulled the crisp white sheets up around his neck and snuggled into the blankets.

"What about the mon…?"

"LeRoy, would you just shut up and git on out of here." He motioned to the door and raised his voice enough to wince from the pressure in his head. In a quieter voice, he said, "You can come pick me up tomorrow morning, okay? We got until tomorrow night to work things out. Don't worry…and keep your mouth shut."

Placated by Pete's words, LeRoy spit into the trash can one last time and walked out the door. He carried his greasy cap in one hand while scratching sand from his scalp with the other.

The doctor left instructions for the nurse to have Mr. Jensen bathed thoroughly. "If he feels like he can handle the shower, make sure he's supervised by an orderly. If he's too dizzy when he stands up, you'll have to do a sponge bath."

Pete wasn't thrilled with the idea of taking a shower, but thought a sponge bath by a good-looking nurse might be fun. As he speculated on that idea, he heard voices outside the door.

"Dr. McCarthy, there's a Sergeant Childers that would like to see you. He was headed this way." There was obvious concern in the duty nurse's voice.

"Hmm, wonder what that's about."

"I think it has something to do with that lady who was lost in the bus wreck a couple of days ago."

Pete slid his legs over the edge of the bed. The floor was cool under his feet and he felt suddenly lightheaded. He took a couple of deep breaths and when he felt steady enough, he shuffled toward the half opened door.

"Good afternoon, Doctor. I'm Sergeant Childers from the sheriff's department in Baker, California. I'm investigating the disappearance of Grace Partain."

"I'm Dr. McCarthy. I thought they took all the people from that wreck on into Las Vegas."

"I think they did, but she wasn't one of them. I know it sounds crazy, but I'm trying to follow every lead or idea that comes to me. I thought maybe she might have had a head injury or amnesia…and maybe someone coming south picked her up and transported her to this hospital."

"I wish I could help, but she didn't show up here. The only head trauma we've had is a guy who was admitted last night."

Pete suddenly felt exposed. Besides the fact that his hospital gown didn't quite meet in the back, he was shocked to become part of a conversation about Grace Partain. Was someone on to his plan? He leaned closer to catch more information. The door flew open with such force he jumped back clumsily.

"Why, Mr. Jensen, I didn't expect to find you out of bed yet." The nurse had a towel and washcloth neatly folded in a basin. "Since you're up, you can just go right in here and take a shower, doctor's orders." She opened the bathroom door, flipped on the light, and ushered Pete inside. Keeping his back to the wall, he shuffled into the small bathroom, regretting that the sponge bath was off.

"I'll send someone to help you."

"No! I can do it myself!" Pete wasn't sure who she might send, but he'd seen a couple of the guys who helped out and they didn't look like anyone he wanted in the shower with him.

CHAPTER 8

Ralph Moore had been a private investigator for thirty years. Retirement was nearing and he was ready for it. His knees bothered him and his blood pressure soared without daily medication. As a kid, he'd worked on his grandfather's cattle ranch, and even then, riding a horse made his knees ache. He was built like a Lego toy; short and stocky with round full limbs that lacked flexibility.

The possible kidnapping of Grace Partain rejuvenated him. He didn't have much information to go on, but the challenge sparked his creativity. The only place to start was at the beginning, the bus wreck. Last week's newspapers gave him information about the wreck, but he didn't rely on them to be factual. He called the Highway Patrol and left a message for Mike Turcell. In moments, the call was returned.

"Officer Turcell here."

"Ralph Moore calling from Las Vegas. I'm a private investigator on the Grace Partain case."

"Grace Partain...the woman missing from the bus wreck?"

"That's the one. I'd like to ask a few questions."

"Okay, but I don't think I'll be much help. I'm on the road toward Baker right now." They agreed to meet in a coffee shop at 5:00 p.m.

Ralph wasn't thrilled about driving to Baker, but he knew Turcell would want to see his credentials before he'd tell him anything. Unlike most investigators, Ralph wasn't an ex-cop and often had a hard time getting the information he needed. In preparation for the interview, he wrote several questions on a yellow legal pad and left space between each one to fill in the answers.

In the Baker Coffee Shop, Turcell and Moore introduced themselves, slid into a booth, and ordered sodas. Ralph added curly fries to the order. He knew it was a no-no, but his wife wasn't there with her incessant warnings.

Officer Turcell took off his sunglasses and hat to expose a buzz haircut, tanned skin, and a face that featured a large nose, flanked by two small eyes, and underlined by a full mustache.

Ralph started at the top of the yellow pad. "What time did you get the call and what do you remember?"

"It was about ten o'clock on Saturday night when the 911 call came in. I was at the coffee shop in Baker and arrived on scene in less than ten minutes. The bus was over the bank on its side. A fire engine with a paramedic arrived moments behind me. The firefighters set up a triage to assess the victims' injuries as well as they could. But there was still an awful sand storm going on and it was impossible to do anything outside of the bus. It was bad inside, too. Most of the windows were busted out."

"Was anyone outside the bus?"

"There were a couple of passengers who weren't hurt badly... they had made their way to the roadside to get help. I nearly ran over them when I got to the wreck. The visibility was about zero. I made them get in the car and stay until I could assess the situation. On my run for the bus, I thought I could see some bodies, but there was too much sand coming horizontally with such force that we couldn't do anything about them right away."

"What was it like inside?" Ralph wasn't sure if any of this information was getting him any clues, but he continued to scribble down notes.

"Lots of confusion. Bodies everywhere. Some people trying to help others get down out of the wind as much as they could…trying to stop cuts from bleeding and calming those who were out of control with fear."

"There were ten killed. Were they all inside the bus?"

Turcell took a moment to think back. "No, I think there were six inside and four outside. By the time the wind died down, there were more firemen and paramedics helping out."

"How did they know someone was missing?"

"They didn't discover that until after everyone had been cared for. I found the passenger list and went through it one by one until only one was not accounted for."

"Did anyone on the bus know her?"

"Hmm, I don't think so. It wasn't until we found her purse outside on the ground that we figured out she was the missing person."

"Did she leave anything on the bus?"

"No. Oh…there was a copy of a John Grisham's book, *The Testament*, wrapped up in a sweater that didn't seem to belong to anyone else. I remember that because I had just read that book and thought it was great."

"Where do you think she went?"

Officer Turcell paused. "I was in charge of the scene and the accident. When I left, the bus driver was unconscious, ten people were dead, three injured were transported into the Las Vegas Hospital, and I assumed Mrs. Partain would be found soon. I thought she probably got out into the sandstorm and got blown down somewhere."

"Do you think it's possible someone took her off the bus?"

"Mr. Moore, I'm afraid I'm going to have to get back on the road. I've told you all I know. I turned the investigation over to the sheriff's department. What they did after that really isn't my concern. Sergeant Childers is the guy you want to talk to."

Ralph quickly thought through all the information, wondering if he'd missed anything. "I appreciate your help. Let me see if I had any other questions…"

"Gotta go. Good luck, sir." Turcell was already on his feet with his hand extended. Ralph gave it a shake and settled back in the booth to look over his notes and eat his curly fries. He made a sketch of the wreck with a few stick figures on the ground around the bus. *Did Grace try to get help by the road and stumble into the hands of a kidnapper? Or was she unconscious on the ground when the kidnapper came upon the wreck and snatched her? If he found her unconscious, he would have had to dodge the law enforcement and emergency services personnel as they arrived. Of course, the blinding sand storm would have offered cover. How could a passerby come up with a plan to kidnap someone out of the blue? It seems like any driver would have been worried about his own safety. The only logical answer was that Grace must have gone to the aid of a stranger seeking help or safety, and whoever it was took advantage of her weakened condition.* Ralph still wanted to talk to someone who had been on the bus.

He hoisted himself out of the booth, paid for the sodas, and headed for the sheriff's substation in Baker. In minutes, he was told Sergeant Childers had gone south on police business and wouldn't return for hours. Ralph talked a young reserve officer into leading him to the accident site for a look. He got out and kicked around the sandy area, but nothing there gave him even an inkling of a clue. In the past, he'd had times when just visiting a crime site seemed to bring whispers of direction to him. It was eerie, but immensely helpful when it happened. After fifteen minutes of nothing but hot wind, the smell of sagebrush, and the sound of cars and trucks thundering by on the highway, he gave up and headed back to Las Vegas.

Phil considered leaving the doorbell unanswered. He was in no mood to face a door-to-door salesperson, or anyone for that matter. Sleep had eluded him all day and the tension of waiting was tearing at his nerves. In his mind, he saw Grace being tortured and taunted. Again and again, he pushed the horrible image from his mind and prayed for her safety.

The doorbell rang impatiently for a second time, and Phil pulled himself from the chair.

"Who's there?" Phil hesitated by the door.

"Sergeant Childers, San Bernardino Sheriff's Department."

Phil unlocked and opened the door. As he ushered Childers inside, his mind was racing. *Why had Childers come all the way to Highland?*

"I'm glad to meet you, but isn't this a bit out of your jurisdiction?"

The sheriff's department was searching for Grace as though she were missing. He couldn't tell them about the kidnapper's call, but what could he say?

"It was a long ride, and it's not out of our jurisdiction. I went to Barstow and figured I might as well come a bit farther and ask you a few questions face-to-face. Besides, my favorite uncle is a pastor here and I haven't dropped in on him in a long time."

"Have you made any headway in finding my wife?"

"I'm sorry to say, we have not. I went to the hospital in Barstow thinking maybe she ended up there. But no."

"Do you think maybe someone took her from the area of the accident?"

"To tell you the truth, I don't know what to think. I thought maybe you could help us." Phil noticed the sheriff's eyes scanning the room as though he suspected something out of the ordinary.

"What could I do to help?" Phil sat on the sofa and offered Sergeant Childers his big chair. Childers perched on the arm, but it was obvious that he didn't intend to stay long.

"Someone called my office and said you and your partner had just withdrawn a large sum of money from your accounts. Is that true?"

Phil tried to stay calm. His heart began to pound, but he breathed deeply, put his head back, and closed his eyes. "We...ah... thought maybe..." His mind was flooded with words that would tumble out incoherently if he didn't check himself carefully. "We thought...perhaps if we...offered a reward...maybe Grace's disappearance would get more notice. Is that okay?"

"I hadn't heard anything about a reward. That's a great idea."

"Yeah, we were going to do that tomorrow. Whatever it takes."

Phil wondered if Childers knew how much money they had withdrawn. If he didn't know, maybe he could offer a small reward above what he had to pay the kidnapper. But if Childers did know the amount and then Phil didn't offer it all, that might cause more suspicion. Phil felt like he was the criminal.

"You said 'we.' Who were you referring to?"

"My partner, Sheldon Hargrave. We had to cash in several of our joint investments."

Childers asked for his phone number and scribbled it on a small pad he pulled from his shirt pocket.

"I'll be talking to the media in the morning, and I'll be glad to go ahead and let them know about the reward. What amount shall I tell them?"

Suddenly Phil got an idea. "How about $50,000? If that doesn't get anything, we're set to offer more. Is that okay?"

"That'll work."

Thinking the conversation was over, Phil stood up, but Childers wasn't done.

"How were you and Grace getting along?"

"Gr—great. Fine. Of course, she's been real busy with the end of school...reports cards, cleaning up her classroom, and all."

"How about friends? Did anyone go along with her on the bus trip?" Childers seemed calm, but Phil caught himself picking at his cuticles and wishing this interview was over.

"No, she went alone. End of school. I guess everyone else had vacation plans. She just needed to get away by herself."

"Did she ever go off on a trip like this by herself before?"

"No, not that I remember. Most of her socializing consists of playing bridge with her three teacher friends."

Childers asked for their names and phone numbers. He jotted them down, gave his condolences to Phil, and headed for the door.

Phil hesitated to shake hands for fear his sweating palms would reveal his nervousness. "That uncle of yours, what's his name?"

"John Troude. He lives about four blocks down. Do you know him?"

"I sure do. He performed our wedding ceremony almost twenty years ago, but I have to admit, I haven't been to church in years."

"Well, he's a great guy and truly has a heart for God. I know you must be at wit's end worrying about your wife. John would be a good one to talk to. He's listened to my problems a few times and was a real help."

Phil wished he could tell Childers about the kidnapper, but he was afraid that police intervention would backfire and cause harm to Grace. "Maybe I'll call him."

"I'll tell him you're going to." Childers stepped off the porch and hurried to his car.

Phil cringed. Now he was committed to advertise a reward with money he had intended to pay off the kidnapper and he would be expected to call Pastor Troude. And what was Sergeant Childers going to ask Fran and the other teachers? He had been so short with Fran when she called, no telling what she was thinking. And Sheldon, what would he say? Or what if Marilyn got into it?

Pete felt certain there had been a mistake. When he got out of the shower, a fresh hospital gown awaited him folded neatly on the back of the toilet. It had big yellow daisies with smiling pink piggies skipping through the pattern. He poked his head out of the door a couple of times and weakly called for help, but no one came. There didn't seem to be any other choice, so he put it on and sneaked toward the bed.

"Well, Mr. Jensen. Did we enjoy our shower?" The duty nurse breezed in just as Pete stooped over to adjust the terrycloth hospital slippers. He grabbed the flaps of the flowered gown and tried to spin around and sit down on the bed at the same time. Off balance, he missed the edge of the bed and slid down to the cold floor.

"Oh, Mr. Jensen, are you okay?" The nurse put both arms out for Pete to use for support. He refused her help and made a spectacle of himself as he floundered on the floor in the flowered gown.

"Please, Mr. Jensen, let me help you." Pete figured it was this woman who had given him the gown with the piggies, and she was probably finding this whole spectacle rather entertaining. With one huge grunt, he got to his feet and fell into bed, pulling the piggies and flowers down to cover what had already been exposed several times.

"Isn't it about time for dinner?" Pete panted as he adjusted the covers.

"Any minute now." The nurse exited, but not fast enough to keep Pete from seeing her hands go up to her mouth and her shoulders begin to shake.

Very funny. All he wanted now was a good hot meal, a restful night's sleep, and tomorrow he'd be ready to get going on his five-hundred-thousand-dollar plan. The flowers and piggies would all be behind him.

Pastor John Troude was thrilled to see his nephew. It was the first time an investigation had led Childers to this area and he savored the moment.

"I hate to break this up, but could I use your phone to make a few calls before it gets too late? Then we can visit a little bit more before I have to leave."

Troude showed him to the phone and left the room.

The conversations were brief, but when he was finished, Childers was satisfied that Marilyn Hargrave was mad at Phil for tying up her money, Fran was mad at Phil because she thought he had something to do with Grace's disappearance, and Sheldon was covering up something. He had admitted to cashing out a half-million dollars' worth of joint investments, but insisted it was earnest money for an offer on a huge property deal.

He told his uncle about investigating the Partain disappearance and about Phil's plans to call on him. Pastor Troude begged Tom to stay overnight rather than make the two-hour drive, but to no avail. They hugged affectionately before parting, and Childers hit the road again.

❦

At work, things got much worse. Grace had eaten a little dinner before they left the house and again, her stomach did a flip. Her wrists hurt and her back ached from the night before and Madeline was watching her every move.

Madeline caught Grace alone in the locker room. "Keep your stinking hands off Jerry, Gloria."

Grace was shocked. "What?" she asked in confusion.

"I don't know where you came from, but I know you're staying with Jerry. He's mine."

"He is? Does he know that?" It slipped out before Grace could stop it.

Madeline slapped her with such force, Grace slammed up against the lockers. Before she could respond, Madeline grabbed her by the hair with both hands and started banging her head against the metal.

Grace had never fought with anyone in her life. As her head was slammed back and forth, she tried to tear Madeline's arms away, but only succeeded in causing herself more pain. With all her force, Grace stomped hard on her attacker's foot and delivered a punch to her stomach.

Madeline released her grip, gasping for breath. After a few seconds, she shrugged and limped toward the door, stopping only briefly. "I'm not finished with you, Gloria. You'd better stay out of my way."

Grace ran her fingers over her scalp checking for lumps or cuts. She couldn't believe she had just been physically attacked. Who could she go to for help? She thought about telling Jerry, but she wasn't sure what his reaction would be. If he and Madeline had something going, he would side with Madeline. How about Sadie? No, she was just a kid. What help could she be? Grace decided she had no alternatives and had to let it go for now.

What would Phil tell her to do? He would be appalled if he knew his schoolteacher wife was brawling in the storeroom of a third-rate casino. There was a time when he would have cared. On the way to celebrate their fifth anniversary, they had a flat tire. While Grace waited in the car, Phil got out to remedy the problem. In minutes, two men in a lowered pickup truck stopped and began to taunt Phil and moved toward Grace's side of the car. Phil came around the front of the car to meet them. With a firm grip on the tire iron and a threatening look on his face, he spoke with authority. "Get away from the car and leave immediately or someone is going to get hurt...bad!" The men only hesitated a second, but it was easy to see that Phil meant business. When they had gone, he finished changing the tire in a rush. He didn't say a word, but he got into the car, took Grace in his arms, and held her until his heart quit pounding. She wondered if Phil's heart was pounding now. Had he even taken any steps to find her?

She reached into her locker to find her comb. Instead, her hand fell on an unfamiliar object. It was a book...a Bible. The cover was thick paper, but inside the front page, in beautiful script was written, "I will never leave thee, nor forsake thee. (Hebrews 13:5) From a friend who cares."

The door flew open. Grace turned quickly to conceal the Bible in the darkness of her locker, but it was too late. "What've you got there?" Madeline reached for the locker door, but Grace stood in her way.

"It's nothing you'd be interested in." Grace leaned against the door concealing the Bible.

"You stole something out of my locker, didn't you?"

"No, of course not. Isn't it locked?" Grace half turned to check Madeline's locker.

"The lock is right here." Madeline dangled the padlock from her finger. "I forgot to lock it."

It was a stand-off. Grace didn't want to let Madeline near her locker, and Madeline wasn't about to go away.

"Get out of my way, now. Let me lock up."

Grace stepped aside while Madeline opened her own locker and felt inside. She patted the contents. First calmly with one hand, then impatiently feeling in and under items with both hands, and then wildly rifling through the locker so a hair brush and two T-shirts fell out on the floor.

"You witch! What have you done with my…stuff?" Madeline demanded, poking Grace in the chest with her index finger. "Hand it over, you thief!"

"I have nothing of yours. Nothing!"

With fire in her eyes, Madeline clinched her fists and bared her teeth in a grimace. Grace planted her feet and prepared to defend herself again.

The door opened and Jerry stuck his head in. "Hey, could we get to work now, ladies? We got customers waiting. Let's hustle up or I'm going to dock your pay!"

Grace had no idea what was missing from Madeline's locker, and wondered why she didn't report it to Jerry, but she wasn't going to hang around to find out. She grabbed her apron and escaped from the room right on Jerry's heels. Approaching the bar, she took out the folded piece of newspaper and threw it in a trash can.

Grace tried to get Sadie's attention a couple of times, but the noise in the casino made it impossible without shouting or moving nearer the person. When she saw Sadie head for the restroom, she followed discretely.

"Hey Gloria! How's it going tonight? Better, I hope."

"I got off to a bad start. What is Madeline's problem?" Grace asked.

"Problems, you mean. Where should I begin?" Sadie replied.

"She accused me of being interested in Jerry and of taking something out of her locker."

"Whew! She'd like to think Jerry cares about her, but Jerry only cares about Jerry. She can get pretty rough."

"You're telling me. She banged my head against the locker a couple of times. I thought she was going to kill me."

"Don't mess with her, and whatever you do, don't tell Jerry. If she got fired, I hate to think what she'd do to you. And Jerry…I know he's into something bad. I've seen him talking to Vito and his buddies. I don't know what he's dealing, but it isn't cards."

"You mean drugs?" Grace was shocked at how far she had come from her world of children, chalkboards, and playgrounds.

"I don't know, but I know those guys are hanging around here for something besides playing slot machines."

Grace noticed a beaded bracelet on Sadie's wrist. The design spelled out WWJD. The same letters she'd seen on the waitress before all this happened.

"Sadie, what does that bracelet mean?"

Sadie twisted the bracelet and hesitated as though she were connecting with its meaning. "The letters WWJD stand for What Would Jesus Do?"

"Why do you wear it?" Grace's question was sincere.

"It reminds me to stop and think about how Jesus would handle things. Sometimes I forget anyway, but I try."

"You do mean the Jesus in the Bible, don't you?"

"The stories of him are in the Bible, but since I invited him into my heart...he's with me all the time."

"Hmm. I used to go to church, but it was a long time ago." Grace was struck by the contrast between the conversation in the locker room and this one in the restroom. *Strange.*

"You didn't happen to open your locker tonight, did you, Gloria?"

"Yes, I did. In fact...oh, so you're the one...I mean, did you put something in my locker?"

"I sure did. I hope it's okay. I just wanted you to have it. I'm sorry it's not fancy leather bound, but..."

"It was very nice of you, Sadie. You don't even know me, but thank you." Grace thought of all the lies she had concocted to get to this point. Sadie would hate her if she knew.

"If you stick around for a while, maybe you can come to church with me. I know you'd like it."

"We'll see. I was thinking about trying to get a bus ticket to Phoenix tomorrow. I can't stay with the Hodges's much longer. He scares me."

"How about staying with me for a while?" Sadie offered.

"I don't have much of anything at Jerry's, but I hate to offend Isabel, his mom. She's been so nice to me."

"Well, the offer is open. You could sleep on the sofa." She quickly scratched her address and phone number on a napkin from her tray and gave it to Grace. "Seriously, Gloria, I'd be glad to have you."

"Thanks, we'll see. We'd better get back to work or we'll both be fired."

CHAPTER 9

Moore tried to sleep, but sleep wouldn't come. He had read and reread last weekend's papers about the bus accident. His interview with Officer Turcell and his visit to the site of the accident helped paint a clearer picture of what happened. But Grace Partain was missing from the scene and he could not figure out how she left the picture.

He silently slipped out of bed, leaving his wife undisturbed. She was used to Ralph's late night comings and goings. He put on some clothes and headed for the hospital. If the accident happened around midnight, this might be the best time to catch the same crew as that of Saturday night. In the hospital parking lot, his knees begged to be back in bed, but he struggled out of the car and hobbled across the parking lot. His gray suit, wrinkled from the perspiration of the day, made Moore look disheveled and unprofessional. It wasn't easy for this stump of a man to be impressive, but he regretted not trying harder.

Dr. Dornan was summoned and Moore found a seat in the waiting room. Thirty minutes passed before the doctor appeared. Introductions were brief and the picture of Grace Partain was produced.

"I already told the sheriff from Baker that I was sure she was here that night. She came in with her mother who had chest pains.

Isabel Hodges. But they left the next morning. She wasn't any part of the bus accident."

When asked about the bus driver, he said he'd been responding to some questions by squeezing the nurse's hand. They were hoping that he would come around, but they were uncertain about the extent of the damage to his brain.

Moore gave his card to Dr. Dornan and asked to be notified if there was any change in the driver's status. Isabel Hodges would have to wait until morning, but Moore had a feeling he was making progress.

The stench of smoke, alcohol, and perspiring gamblers mixed together was a sickening combination that sent Grace retching to the front door for fresh air again and again. The bartender gave her some saltines to nibble and that helped only temporarily. She thought about sneaking back to the locker room and lying down on the wooden bench for a few minutes, but she was afraid Madeline would corner her again. Each tray full of drinks got heavier and heavier as the night wore on. The ringing bells and clanking coins formed a cacophony that blurred her thinking. Her head pounded, her eyes burned, and her stomach churned.

"Hey, lady, I need a drink over here! How about a vodka and tonic?" someone shouted.

"Over here! Get me a whiskey sour!"

"Gloria!" Jerry headed in her direction. "Get a move on. What's the hold up?"

Grace lifted her eyes and everything moved in slow motion. There was Phil, coming through the front door, headed right toward her. His face was full of love as he opened his arms to embrace her. She went to him as though she were slogging through wet clay with clumps of it clinging to her shoes. He enfolded her in his arms and she basked in the security of his presence.

"Gloria! What's your problem?" Grace looked up into Jerry's face. He was standing over her as she lay on the carpet, but he made no move to assist her. The room was spinning and Grace just wanted to curl up and die.

Suddenly Sadie was kneeling by her side. "Gloria…Gloria. Can you hear me?"

Grace wanted to answer. She even thought she did say something, but no sound came out of her mouth.

Sadie fanned her with the note pad she used to write down orders. Grace couldn't make herself move, but she was aware of Jerry asking for a glass of water. She tried to muster strength, but for what? Where was she going? She had no place to go. No one to love. No life to live. For a fleeting moment, she saw Phil and she felt his love, but it was only an illusion caused by whatever malady had beset her.

The water splashed across her face. "There, that ought to get you on your feet." This was Jerry's idea of helping.

"Oh, thanks, Jerry," Sadie said sarcastically as she lifted Grace to a sitting position and patted the water away with a napkin.

Grace tried to shake off the dazed feeling. Using Sadie to steady herself, she slowly got to her feet. What now? Should she beg Jerry to let her lie down for a while or take her back to the house?

"Take her to the locker room. I've got business to attend to. I'll take her to the house in a little while." Jerry went back to the bar with his business associates.

Grace feared being left alone in the locker room after being attacked by Madeline.

"Do you think you'll be all right?" Sadie had folded a few towels on the bench and tried to make Grace as comfortable as possible. She got a glass of water for Grace, but she was afraid to be absent from the casino for more than a few minutes.

"I think so. I'm feeling a little better now. I just hope Madeline doesn't come in."

Sadie was only gone for a few minutes when Madeline came in swearing angrily. Grace was curled up on the bench with her back to the door, but playing possum wouldn't work with Madeline.

"What did you do with the coke, Gloria?" She loomed over Grace with a look of rage.

"I...I...I don't drink Coke," Grace answered weakly. "All this over a missing soft drink?"

"I'm not talking about Coke you drink, you idiot," she hissed through clenched teeth. "I'm talking about the baggy of cocaine that was in my locker!" Madeline's legs were almost touching the bench. Her fists were clinched so tight her knuckles were white. There were dark patches of perspiration soaking through the underarm of her red satin cowboy shirt.

"Cocaine! I've never even seen it except in the movies." Grace stayed in the fetal position hoping to protect herself by rolling up like a sow bug if there was trouble. She was no match for Madeline.

"Give it up, Gloria. Don't give me that goody-two-shoes crap. Where is the stuff?"

I will never leave thee nor forsake thee. Grace could almost hear the audible words come to her in a still small voice.

"I don't have it, Madeline. I didn't come here to hurt anyone or steal anything. I just..."

Madeline yanked Grace's locker open and dug through the contents wildly. She cursed and threw each item down when it yielded nothing.

"You must have it on you somewhere!" She tore at Grace's shirt pocket as Grace tried to keep her from it. Then rolling her from side to side, she dug her fingers into each jean pocket. The jeans were tight and Grace felt Madeline's fingers digging at her skin through the pocket.

"Give it up. I won't quit until I find that baggy. I don't care if I have to strip you down!" Her face was red with fury. She pulled one of Grace's tennis shoes off, examined it quickly and tossed it across the room where it hit a bottle of cleaning solution and sent it crashing into the sink.

"You won't find anything on me. I don't want anything you have."

With that, Madeline took a broom from the corner and brought the handle down with all her force across Grace's head and shoulder. Grace tried to protect herself with her arms. Madeline left muttering, "Jerry was depending on me to keep it safe, and now it's gone. He'll kill me." Grace whimpered and touched her fingers to the split in her forehead.

When Sadie came back to check on Grace, she gasped at the sight. A lump on Grace's forehead oozed blood down over her right eye and she cowered at the sound of the door opening.

Sadie put her arms around her shoulders. "Oh my goodness. What happened?"

"Ooh," Grace moaned from the pain in her bruised shoulder. "Madeline hit me with the broom handle. She accused me of stealing cocaine from her. As she left, I thought she said something about keeping it for Jerry."

Sadie didn't hesitate. "Come on. Let's get out of here before they both come back."

The sun was coming up when Sadie pulled the car up in front of the Hodges's house. "Just get your stuff and hustle. Jerry will be here soon."

Grace's head was pounding, but she moved as quickly as she could. Inside the house, she gathering up her few belongings, snatched the torn newspaper out from between the mattress, and headed for the front door.

"Gloria?"

Grace whirled around, startled. "Isabel! You scared me."

"Oh my...what happened to your forehead?"

"I fell at work...one of the girls is taking me to the hospital."

Isabel moved closer. "Where's Jerry?"

"He's still at work. He was really busy, so I got a ride."

"Why didn't you go straight to the hospital?" Isabel didn't seem like the same gullible woman Grace had helped a few days earlier.

"I...I...I wanted a change of clothes. This red satin shirt..." Grace tried to tuck her small bundle together.

"Here, let me help you." She reached for the bundle and the newspaper fell to the floor.

"What's the newspaper for?"

"It...it...was an old one I had in my room yesterday." Grace edged toward the door.

"We didn't get a paper yesterday, remember Gloria?" Isabel picked it up and started to open the pages.

"Oh yeah, I guess I...picked that one up at the store."

"Let's see. Are you sure this isn't...? What's this?" Isabel looked through the hole in the front page.

"I really need to go now, Isabel. My head is killing me." Grace slipped out the door and down the walk. She knew Isabel would question the missing article, but it would take her awhile to figure out what it was about.

"What took so long?" Sadie pulled the car away from the curb.

"Jerry's mom caught me at the door."

"I was afraid Jerry would come home."

"Me, too." Grace pulled the car's visor down and was shocked at her image in the mirror. The lump on her forehead was multicolored with blood smeared from the cut, around her eye, and down her cheek.

"I don't think you ought to go back there. If Jerry thinks you had something to do with lifting his stash, you may be in big trouble."

Grace put her head back on the seat. She wondered if Jerry would come after her. And if he did, what would he do to her? Would he try to beat information out of her, information she didn't have? Where would she be safe? Her thoughts turned to Phil. What had he been doing all this time? If she called him, would he drop everything and come after her? Would he forgive her for running off and doing such a stupid thing? She decided to call him as soon as she was finished at the hospital.

The TV blared all night, rivaled only by Pete's raucous snoring. The nurse had checked in several times, but Pete never moved. He had never been so clean and comfortable in his life.

"Grace Partain disappeared from a turnaround bus tour on Saturday..." Whether it was the recognition of the name mentioned by the news commentator on the TV or the smell of the breakfast tray being delivered, Pete's eyes flew open and he was suddenly wide awake.

The reporter continued, "Although searchers have been called off, Mr. Partain is offering a fifty-thousand dollar reward to anyone who provides information that leads to Mrs. Partain's safe return. Anyone who has information should contact the San Bernardino Sheriff's Department."

Pete was confused. Why would Partain be offering a reward? Was he trying to foul up the whole deal? Fifty thousand was a lot of money. No telling what nut might try to collect it. Pete thought about calling the San Bernardino Sheriff and telling them he'd found Grace's driver's license. Maybe they'd give him a part of the reward for turning it over. Another fifty thousand would be a nice addition to the half-million he'd soon collect.

He dumped the poached egg out of the bowl onto the thick pancakes, covered them with syrup, and gobbled up the entire creation. The reward news hadn't hurt his appetite. He slurped down the hot coffee, following it with grape juice and six prunes.

Dr. McCarthy entered the room. "So how do you feel this morning?"

"Slept like a baby and can't wait to get on the road." Pete clasped his hands behind his head and put his hairy elbows out to each side on the puffy white pillow. "Hate to leave your fine establishment, but if it's all the same to you, I'll call LeRoy to come pick me up as soon as I have another cup of coffee and some hash browns." He belched loudly and Dr. McCarthy stepped back a bit.

"Let me check your head and run a couple of simple tests and I'll make the decision." Dr. McCarthy was swift and thorough. He shined a light into each of Pete's eyes and looked closely. Then he had Pete follow his finger from side to side and seemed satisfied. "Okay, Mr. Jensen, you will be released as soon as someone arrives to assist you."

"But what about my coffee and hash browns?" Pete frowned disappointedly. "I'm not leavin' 'til I get 'em."

When Jerry arrived home, Isabel was waiting anxiously. She swung the screen door open before he got out of the car.

"Is Gloria here?" Jerry pushed by Isabel and tromped through the house taking a quick look in every room.

"Not now, but she did stop by."

Jerry didn't bother to look at his mother. He entered Grace's room and saw that everything was gone. Isabel followed him as he continued his search.

"Where'd she go?"

"To the hospital, I think."

"The hospital? What for?"

"Didn't you see her?"

"Of course I saw her. But she left without telling me, and I was looking all over for her. That's why I'm late."

"She was going to have a doctor look at that cut."

Jerry quit pacing abruptly and looked hard at Isabel. "What cut?"

"She said she had a fall at work. Her forehead was cut and there was blood smeared down the side of her face."

"A fall? She blacked out or fainted or something, but she didn't cut herself. I was right beside her." Jerry was trying to figure out what could have caused the cut. He knew there was no cut when he threw the glass of water in her face or when he sent her to the locker room with Sadie. Later, Madeline had gone to the locker room to get the coke she had been keeping for him. When she came back, she was shaken. She told him Gloria had stolen the baggie and she hoped he'd kill her for it. He went to the locker room, but nobody was there. Back in the casino, there was no sign of Gloria, Sadie, or Madeline. He wondered if the trio had run off with his stash?

"I'm going to the hospital." Jerry noticed the folded paper on the table. "Where did you get that newspaper? Today's is out on the walk."

Isabel opened it up and suddenly realized the main article was torn out. "That's strange. This is the missing paper from yesterday, but one of the front-page articles are gone. Gloria had it in her room."

Jerry rushed out the door.

"Hey, Jerry, where are you going?"

"To the hospital. If I don't find Gloria there, I'm going to Madeline's."

Isabel walked back to the kitchen, turned on the TV, and poured herself some juice.

"Mr. Partain is offering a large reward for information…"

Nausea hit Grace as they entered the hospital. Sadie hurried to the cafeteria and brought back toast and a glass of milk while Grace waited patiently. She was the only one in the emergency room. By the time she finished the milk and toast, the doctor was ready to stitch the cut. Two sutures and they were on their way.

"Sadie, I've got something I have to tell you."

"Well, I've got something to tell you, too."

Grace shut her eyes. "I can't go back to Jerry's house or the casino. I think we're in danger."

"I know. I'm taking you to my apartment."

"I have something else to…tell…you." Grace's voice faded and Sadie realized she was sound asleep.

Phil was a wreck. Sleeping fitfully all night, he dreamed that Grace walked into the bedroom and caressed his hair. He woke to the stillness of the house and his heart sank. Nightmares of a man tormenting Grace interrupted his sleep repeatedly and he would wake with a start, sweating, his heart racing. Then he lay awake, desperate for rest and afraid to sleep. His mind moved rapidly from one "what if" scenario to another. *What if Ralph Moore didn't get any leads or the kidnappers didn't show up at the appointed time and place? What if Childers was still suspicious? What if Sheldon heard the news about the reward and thought Phil had turned the tables on him? What if the kidnapper heard about the reward and thought his plan was thwarted? What if Grace was already dead?* He tried to clear his mind, but it was impossible. His stomach was in knots from drinking too much coffee and only occasional snacks for three days. His muscles were stiff and sore from lack of exercise.

Phil turned on the TV in the bedroom with the remote, too tired to leave the bed. Almost instantly, there was the photo of Grace and news of the reward offered for any information leading to her return. Childers certainly hadn't wasted any time.

CHAPTER 10

Jerry was determined to catch up with Gloria before Madeline did. If she had the coke, he could take it back, make the deal, and swear to Madeline that Gloria got away with it. If she didn't have it, then he'd go after Madeline with a vengeance. What he couldn't figure out was what happened to Gloria to send her to the hospital in the first place.

When he asked for Gloria Franklin, the emergency nurses remembered her, but nobody knew where she had gone after she was treated. He headed for Madeline's house. She had left work early, and there was a good chance she still had the stuff. Maybe she was trying to make the sale without him. If Gloria had taken the stash, she probably wouldn't go directly to the local hospital. Maybe she and Madeline got into it over the drugs. Either way, he'd make sure neither of them got another chance to rip him off. It had been a while since he'd needed the pistol he kept under the car seat, but this time he intended to use it if he had to.

Moore saw the wrinkled face peeking through the blinds as though expecting someone. He parked, hobbled up the walk, and rang the bell. A few seconds went by before the door cracked slowly open.

"Good morning. I'm Ralph Moore." He peered around the door until Isabel showed her face.

"Yes?"

"I need to ask you a few questions?"

"Are you the police?" She didn't open the door any farther.

"No, I'm a private investigator. I'm investigating the disappearance of Grace Partain."

That seemed to catch Isabel's interest. "I saw the photo this morning and the news of the reward."

"Have you ever seen that woman before?"

Isabel opened the door a bit wider, but didn't ask Moore to come in.

"I saw a woman who looked very much like her, but her name wasn't Grace Partain."

Moore pulled his notepad from his inside jacket pocket. "What was her name?"

"Her name was Gloria Franklin, and she came to my rescue in one of the casinos on Saturday night."

"Came to your rescue?"

Isabel pushed the screen open and motioned Moore to enter. Moore was certain that he was getting close to finding Grace, but if Isabel was a kidnapper, why would she answer his questions, or let him enter the house?

Isabel ushered Moore into the kitchen and offered him a cup of coffee. He saw the hazelnut creamer that he loved sitting on the counter and quickly accepted.

He made himself comfortable at the red-topped table with chrome legs, something left over from the fifties. An olive green ceramic pot held yellow and orange plastic daisies that were faded with age.

Isabel poured the coffee, added a generous amount of creamer, and began describing her adventure at the casino. Moore realized Isabel was hungry for a good listener, but he was also hungry for information.

"I was in one of the larger casinos Saturday night, when I got the awfullest chest pain. I fell to the floor and Gloria came to my rescue."

"What time was that?"

"It must have been around eight o'clock. I kind of lost track of time."

"Did she say anything about catching a bus?" Moore sipped the sweetened coffee.

"No, she did go outside to check for her ride...yes, wait a minute, the next morning she told me she had flown to Las Vegas and was waiting for some friends who were traveling to Phoenix, where she was from, and they were supposed to pick her up. That's it. When they didn't come, she was considering trying to get a flight back."

"Did she fly back?"

"No, when she was helping me, someone stole her purse and she ended up with no money."

Moore took another drink of the coffee, trying to put things in order. If it was Grace, she had come by bus and lived in Highland. How could this be the same person? It didn't make any sense.

He continued, "Did you hear about the bus wreck that happened that night?"

"Yes, but not until the next morning. I was pretty much out of it all night and didn't even realize they had brought the hurt people into the hospital."

"Did she say anything about a husband?"

"Yes, she said she was divorced and had two adult children living back east somewhere, I believe."

Moore scratched his baldhead. None of it made any sense. "Did she say she was a teacher?"

"No, she said something about just finishing a job shooting a documentary in Arizona." Eager to continue her story, Isabel went on,

"I invited her to come and stay a few days. After all, she had missed her ride and lost her purse on account of me. She had no money and no place to stay, and I figured she could work for my son."

"I don't get it." Moore pulled out the clipping from the newspaper with Grace's photo. "When you saw this photo, didn't you ask her about it?"

"No, I just saw that photo on TV a few minutes before you came. They were telling about the reward."

"What about the Monday paper and all the times it was on TV on Sunday while the news was hot?"

Now it was Isabel's turn to look puzzled. "Hmm, well on Sunday, Gloria and I came home in a taxi. She insisted I rest all day. We had the TV on for a while, but she seemed kind of nervous, overturned one of my vases, and frankly, I think she needed the quiet. Then Monday morning, for some reason, we didn't get a pa...wait a minute." She got up and rushed into the living room, retrieving the newspaper Grace had left. Shaking it open, she realized it was the Monday paper and there was a big hole in the center. She went back to the kitchen holding the paper out for Ralph.

"Mr. Moore, this may be why I didn't see her photo until now. She somehow kept the paper from us."

"So what else happened?"

Isabel went on to describe how Gloria had gone to work for Jerry. He wrote down the address of the casino and jotted more notes.

"Where is she now?"

"Last I saw of her, she came in this morning with a big bloody lump on her forehead, looked terrible, got her stuff, and headed for the hospital."

"Did she say what happened?"

"She said she fell down. My son came home shortly after and he was real concerned about her. He is a wonderful person, and he wouldn't want anyone to get hurt in his casino. Said he was going to the hospital to check on her and bring her home right away."

Moore finished his coffee and lifted his thick body from the chair. "Guess I'll head over to the hospital."

Isabel stood and blocked his way. "You might as well wait right here. I'm sure he'll be back soon."

"I can't wait."

The phone rang. Phil noticed his shaking hand as he reached for the receiver. This was the big day, and he was scared. The ringing phone set his nerves jangling. Maybe it was Ralph Moore with some news.

"Hello." Phil didn't answer with his usual salesman's voice that welcomed each person as a potential customer.

"Pastor John Troude here. Is this Phil Partain?"

"Yes, sir. It is."

"Do you remember me?"

"Yes, sir. You married Grace and me, didn't you?"

Pastor Troude chuckled. "I sure did. I remember that day especially because of the problems with the flowers."

Phil remembered Grace's upset over the late arrival of the flowers. The service was about to begin and still no florist. Finally, the pastor's wife dashed outside and picked handfuls of flowers from the church garden. As each attendant marched up the aisle, she placed a bunch of flowers in their hands. Tears sparkled on Grace's cheeks as she stepped into view. Always the lady, she smiled bravely as her gloved hands clutched her father's arm. Before she could take a step, a frazzled florist thrust a gorgeous bouquet into her arms.

When all the eyes of the guests were focused on Grace at the back of the church, the florist's assistant entered from the front with two standing baskets of flowers, placed them on either side of the podium and disappeared. Grace was a vision of beauty. Every eye followed her to the front, and though some registered surprise at seeing the baskets, Grace's loveliness overpowered them.

"Mrs. Troude was such a help! If it hadn't been for her, I think Grace might have fallen to pieces."

"Oh, I doubt it. She looked pretty determined to become your wife that day, regardless of the flowers. Speaking of Grace, I've been watching the news. I've been praying for both of you. Is there any news?"

"No, sir. None so far." Phil felt a flood of emotion. "I don't know what to do. But I appreciate your prayers."

"I have to drop some papers at the church. Could I come by for a few minutes?"

Phil had no idea of how to face the day. Although it was early morning, all he could think of was the drive to Las Vegas with the ransom money. Yet, he felt compelled to meet with Pastor Troude. "Sure, that would be great." He gave directions and hung up the phone feeling surprisingly cheered and looking forward to the visit.

Outside the Barstow Hospital, Pete and LeRoy climbed into the tow truck, ignoring the squeal of rusty hinges. Except for a little dizziness, Pete felt good. The clean bed, sleep, and good food had perked him up. LeRoy, on the other hand, was anxious to have Pete talk more about the ransom plan and how it would work.

Pete was still trying to figure out why Partain would be offering a reward. He needed some time to think about it, but without knowing who knocked him over the head, he decided they'd better stay out of the bar. They sat in the hospital parking lot for a long time trying to figure out what to do.

"We got about twelve hours to kill and a three-hour drive. What the heck should we do?" Pete didn't want to sit around twiddling his thumbs all day.

"I only got two bucks. You got any money?" LeRoy asked.

"Nope. About two bucks, like you. How 'bout let's go see yer Ma 'n' talk her outta some dough."

"Ah, Pete. I hate askin' Ma to give us money. She's near spent from workin'. Barely makes ends meet."

"We ain't gonna ask her to GIVE us the money. It'll be a loan. Tomorrow we'll pay her back twice over!" Pete started the tow truck and they headed toward LeRoy's house.

Sadie's one-bedroom apartment was clean and neat, but every space was filled with furnishings and decorations. A knickknack shelf held a collection of angels. Grace could see a whole shelf of fragile handblown glass angels with wispy wings, halos, and flyaway hair. On the shelf above were cherubs, cupid-type angels made of white clay with potbellies and wings that would never have been aerodynamically sound. Little cutesy pictures adorned the walls with sayings about love and charity.

Grace's head throbbed. Sadie put a pillow behind her and helped her get comfortable on the sofa.

"We need to talk…but can we sleep first?" asked Grace.

"Sure thing." It had been a long night for both of them. Sadie went into her bedroom and without even undressing, she lay across the bed and fell asleep.

Jerry shoved the pistol into his waistband and walked toward Madeline's apartment. He recognized her vehicle in the carport and knew she was there. At the door, he knocked a couple of times and took a deep breath. Madeline opened the door a little, but when she saw Jerry, she tried to slam it closed again. Jerry stuck his foot in the way, and grabbing Madeline by the wrist; forcing the door open, he pushed her back into the apartment.

"Ouch! Jerry, you're hurting me!" Madeline fell back onto an overstuffed chair as Jerry released his grip.

"Why did you leave the casino?"

"I…I was scared." Madeline rubbed her wrist and pulled her cotton robe around her.

"I'll give you something to be scared about! Where is my stuff?"

"I swear, Jerry, I don't have it. I think your friend Gloria took it out of my locker."

"What makes you think so?" Jerry leaned over Madeline threateningly.

"She and Sadie got real chummy right away. And I think they left together."

"How did Gloria get her head cut?"

"I don't know. Didn't she fall down in the casino?"

"Yeah, but she didn't cut herself. Did you hit her with something?"

"No way. And if she says I did…or brings the cops into this, I'm gonna tell them it's your stuff."

Jerry wrestled the gun from his waistband and pointed it at Madeline. "That stuff is worth $40,000 dollars. I know you have it somewhere."

Madeline was trembling now. "Come on, Jerry. You know I wouldn't hold out on you. Haven't I always given you everything you've wanted? I'll go with you to find Gloria and Sadie. Come on. When we find them, I bet we'll find the coke."

Chapter 11

Phil opened the door as the bell was still ringing. "Pastor Troude, come on in." The pastor was over six feet tall with impressive shoulders that had not slumped with age. Phil had heard that Troude had been quite a wrestler in college. His closely cropped gray hair somehow made him look younger than his years.

Troude shook Phil's hand warmly. "It's so nice to see you. Thank you for letting me come by."

"No, I thank you for coming by, sir."

"Let's just drop the sir, please. John will be fine. I was sorry to hear about your wife."

Phil removed the mounting pile of newspapers from the sofa and offered the pastor a place to sit. He was too nervous to sit down himself and he leaned against the counter top.

"This ordeal has been terrible. I've hardly slept. I just keep hoping someone will find Grace soon." Phil ran his hand through his hair. Usually every hair was sprayed firmly into place. Today, it felt greasy and unkempt. His hand moved to his unshaven face and he realized that he must be quite a scruffy looking character. "Yeah, I must look pretty rough."

"Well, yes. But it's to be expected considering what you've been going through. How can I help?"

Phil relaxed into his big leather chair, closed his eyes and let his mind wander. "I remember the day of our wedding when the flowers didn't show up. You were so calm. In fact, as we stood in the front of the church watching your wife handing out bunches of uprooted flowers from her garden, I remember you saying a simple prayer... something about...ah...'the flowers may fall, but the word of the Lord never changes.' And presto, the florist appeared in the nick of time."

Troude chuckled. "That comes from a verse in First Peter."

"If there is another verse that could bring Grace back, I wish you'd say it right now."

"Phil, it doesn't quite work that way. My faith and trust is in the Lord Jesus Christ. The Bible says his word will not come back void. That means if I include his words in my prayer, God hears me and things happen."

"Do your prayers always get answered?"

"Absolutely. Sometimes he says, 'Yes.' Sometimes he says, 'No,' and sometimes he says, 'Wait.' I have to have faith that whatever his answer, it will be his plan for me. If I could just have God do whatever I wanted, he would be like a genie and I would be the master. That wouldn't work. I'd make a terrible mess out of things." Pastor Troude smiled widely.

"How do you know what to pray?" Phil was intrigued.

"In the past couple of days, I find myself just talking to God. That's just what he wants you to do, too. Just talk to him. He created us to have fellowship with him."

"I sure haven't had much fellowship with him in the past twenty years. I was making plenty of money and I didn't really see much need for religion." Phil leaned across the footstool, opened the cabinet under the collection of trophies, and pulled out a Bible from under a pile of books.

"Making lots of money will never measure up to having the love of God. It will never fulfill your soul like he will. Money...you can't take it with you. But Jesus...well, if you have him in your heart, you are promised eternal life."

"Sunday is our biggest day in real estate, so going to church is almost impossible."

"It's not about going to church. Asking Jesus to come into your heart can be done anywhere, any day. And when you commit your life to him, he's with you always."

Phil couldn't believe he was listening with such openness. He'd refused to go to church with Grace and she had given up asking him long ago. But all of a sudden, he hungered for something or someone to stop the aching in his heart.

"Pastor Troude, I'm feeling really stupid all of a sudden. But what do I have to do to be...ah, is it called saved or born again or ah...turn myself into a Christian?"

Troude laughed a joyful laugh. "First, you can't turn yourself into a Christian. Pardon me for laughing, but that just struck me funny. It doesn't make any difference what you call it, all you have to do is go to God in prayer, admit that you are a sinner, ask for forgiveness, accept Jesus as your Savior, and invite him into your heart. Jesus has already paid the ransom for your sins when he shed his blood on the cross."

"Ransom? What do you mean?"

Pastor Troude reached for the Bible in Phil's hand. "Ransom is the price paid to get back a person who is held as a slave."

"I know what you mean." Phil thought of Grace.

"Because we were slaves to sin, a ransom had to be paid for us. That ransom was the death of a sinless person. Jesus, the perfect one, paid our ransom. It says in Matthew 20:28..." He thumbed deftly through the delicate pages. "The son of man did not come to be served, but to serve, and to give his life as a ransom for many."

"Whew, he died for me?" Phil could feel a lump in his throat. He felt sorry for all the time he had avoided God and made work his first priority. Now he would almost die himself to get Grace back.

It was silent in the room. Phil was afraid to speak. How could he approach God when he had been so self-indulgent for so long? What gave him the right to even talk to Jesus when he wasn't even willing to tell Pastor Troude the truth about Grace? How could he start to get right with God? How could he speak with a lump the size of Brooklyn in his throat?

Pastor Troude broke the silence. "So, what are you thinking, Phil?"

After a long sigh, Phil's voice came out weak and raspy. "I'm thinking, I don't know where to start."

"Let's start right here and make this your day of salvation." Pastor Troude slid off the sofa and on to his knees. "You don't have to get down on your knees, but I like to." Phil knelt beside him.

"I'll pray the words and you can say them after me...or you can just pray by yourself."

Phil felt his eager heart anticipating a rush of some kind. "You go ahead. I wouldn't know the exact words to say."

"There are no exact words. God knows your heart. We'll just talk to him together." Pastor Troude said his rendition of the Sinner's Prayer and Phil repeated it after him. Before they said "amen," Pastor Troude paused and asked Phil if there was anything he wanted to say to the Lord. Phil felt no embarrassment, but a perfect calm. He told him how sorry he was for turning his back for so many years. After a moment, he continued, "Please forgive me for lying to so many people about Grace's disappearance. Amen."

Phil wiped tears from his bristly cheek.

"Well, Phil. This is your New Birth Day. June the twenty-fifth. The Bible calls it being Born Again."

"June 25. Hey, this is Grace's birthday, too. I can't wait to see her tonight."

Pastor Troude frowned in confusion. "What do you mean... tonight? I thought you hadn't had any news about her disappearance."

"If God can forgive me, I hope you can, too. I know where Grace is."

"You do?" Troude almost shouted as his face lit up.

"Well, kind of. She was kidnapped from the wreck and I'm supposed to go to Las Vegas tonight and pay her ransom."

"Ransom! Why didn't you tell my nephew?"

"I was afraid I'd put Grace in danger. The kidnapper said he'd kill her if I went to the police."

"What time do you have to be there?"

Phil felt relieved to have someone to share this burden with. "Ten o'clock."

"Do you have any clues about the kidnapper?"

"No, but I have a private detective working on it. I haven't heard from him, but he knows where the meeting is tonight."

"I'm going with you."

"Pastor Troude, that might be dangerous. I can't let you do that."

Troude thumbed through the scriptures again. "Look here, in Second Timothy, it says, 'God has not given us the spirit of fear, but of power, and of love and a sound mind.' So, having no fear, and being of sound mind, I'm going with you."

Pete knew he could talk Mamie Ratcliff out of a few bucks. She would gladly sacrifice a few dollars just to get him and LeRoy out of the house. Long hours of waitressing at the truck stop wore her out, and all she wanted to do when she got home was kick back in the recliner and watch television.

"Hey, Mamie. How's it goin'?" Pete turned on the charm.

"What d'ya want, Pete?" Mamie turned up the TV.

"Don't want nothin'. Just thought maybe you'd like to invest a few bucks into a money-makin' concern."

"Invest, is it? Hmmm. This concern wouldn't be a carton of cigarettes and a six pack of beer, would it?"

"Heck, no! We got lot bigger fish to fry. We're makin' a run to Vegas tonight and we're comin' back with a bundle like you ain't never seen. Send us off with some scratch and we'll double it back to ya by tomorra'. Whatdya say?"

"I say you're nuts, Pete. What are you up to now? You ain't gonna get my LeRoy into no trouble are ya?"

Pete took his cap off, trying to register surprise. "Where in the world would you get an idea like that?"

Mamie shook her head and turned the TV up a little louder. Then she waved the remote at LeRoy, who was leaning out the screen door to spit.

"LeRoy, don't you go gettin' into trouble with another one of Pete's hair-brained schemes."

The two men shuffled around behind Mamie's recliner like children who wanted to ask about some forbidden subject. Pete jabbed LeRoy in the ribs and tried to coerce him into broaching the subject of money with his mom. He rubbed his thumb and fingers together to signal "money" and then shoved LeRoy toward the chair. LeRoy drew back and knit his brows together angrily. Pete glared at him and tried to silently scare him into action by wadding up his fist and shaking it in LeRoy's face. When he could see LeRoy was standing firm in his refusal, he stepped up beside the chair to get Mamie's attention.

"So, Mamie, can we count on you for a few bucks of up-front money, just to get started?"

"LeRoy, get him outta here, would'ja? My purse is on the kitchen table. Take a ten if ya really need it."

Pete tried not to act too anxious as he followed LeRoy into the kitchen. "Thanks, Mamie. You won't be sorry." LeRoy pulled her wallet out of the purse and opened it. As he slid out a ten, Pete dug in behind it and plucked out a twenty. When LeRoy tried to snatch it out of his fingers, Pete quickly stuffed it in his pocket with one hand while he put his other forefinger to his lips and motioned for LeRoy to keep still.

"Come on, LeRoy. Let's get goin' and let your mom rest." He pushed LeRoy, who was protesting weakly, out the front door. As the TV blasted away, Pete yelled back, "Pay ya back tomorrow."

Moore headed for the hospital again. He felt like he was running in circles. This time he was sure that he was on the right track, but when he found no Gloria or Grace at the hospital, he called Isabel.

"Is there any other place where I might find your son...or this Gloria?"

"I have no idea about Gloria. She was riding with another person, but I don't know who. Jerry said he was going to check the hospital and then go see his friend Madeline, one of the waitresses, at her apartment."

Moore wondered if Isabel understood any of what was going on. She certainly didn't seem to be covering anything up.

"Do you happen to know the address?"

"Yes, but I'm not sure I should give it to you. You're not going to cause any problems for my son, are you?"

"Of course not. In fact, if he can help me locate this Gloria or Grace or whoever she is, I'll bet the authorities will be thinking you deserve the fifty thousand dollars in reward money."

"Do you think so?" Isabel's voice jumped an octave.

"I sure do."

"Well, if you think it might be helpful...Madeline called here one night when her car was broken down and wanted Jerry to give her a ride. He was gone somewhere, so I went over and gave her a lift. It's 285 Winslow Street, over near the library."

"Thank you so much. You've been very helpful."

"Mr. Moore, if you catch up with this Grace or Gloria, I will... ah...you will see that...ah...I mean, that will entitle me to the fifty thousand dollar reward, won't it?"

"If we find this Grace Partain, I'll make sure the authorities know how you helped."

Things were coming together. It was time for Moore to call Phil and report his progress. A trip to Madeline's would surely make sense of the scattered pieces. Moore dropped some coins in the hospital pay phone. The tiny corner stool wouldn't accommodate Moore's oversized derriere, so he stood, tapping his fingers on the machine. Ten rings, no answer.

Moore left the hospital and drove to the nearest hamburger stand with a drive-thru, getting two burgers, two large orders of fries, and a jumbo cola. This was his diet when his wife wasn't available as his nutritionist.

With a napkin, Moore wiped the last evidence of greasy fries from his lips, wadded up the wrappers, stuffed them into the bag and discarded the whole thing into the trash receptacle in the parking lot. *That was a nice little snack. Now I'm ready to get back to work.*

Okay, Madeline, whoever you are. I hope you have some answers.

Jerry shoved Madeline toward the door. He seemed to delight in terrorizing her with the gun. Shaking it menacingly, he shouted. "Vito is meeting me later and if I don't have the smack, I'm dead. And if we don't get it from Sadie and Gloria, you're dead! Let's go."

Madeline opened the door and met face-to-face with Ralph Moore.

"You must be Madeline." He pushed hard against the door, which swung inward and hit Jerry, knocking the gun to the floor.

"What's this?" Moore acted like he was going to reach down and pick up the gun, but kicked it across the hardwood floor instead. It disappeared under the sofa, out of sight and out of reach.

"Hey, who are you?" Jerry demanded.

Moore pulled out his identification and introduced himself. He tried to stay focused on his investigation concerning Grace Partain, but he knew he had stumbled on to something more than a missing person.

"If you'll just answer a few questions for me, I'll be on my way. Take a seat." Moore pulled up a dining room chair and sat on it backward with his arms propped up on the back. Madeline and Jerry sat on the sofa scowling at one another. Every time Moore looked away, Jerry peeked over the sofa, hoping to glimpse the gun.

When Moore mentioned that Jerry's mother had given him the address, Jerry groaned and rolled his eyes. "That stupid old woman can sure shoot her mouth off!" He leaned over as if to tie his shoes, but while he was down there, he ran his hand along the dust ruffle feeling for the gun.

"She was interested in helping you get the reward."

Jerry sat up straight. "What reward?"

"The fifty-thousand dollars offered for Grace Partain's safe return."

Jerry's expression turned from anger to interest and he forgot about the gun. "Okay, let's talk."

Pete stopped for gas before leaving Barstow and talked LeRoy into handing over the ten he'd borrowed from his mother. He used ten of the twenty he'd taken for more gas and kept ten for himself.

The truck started up with a cough, two backfires, and a cloud of black smoke. At last they were off to Las Vegas to collect the ransom.

The sun was overhead and the temperature on the forty-foot thermometer in Baker registered at 105 degrees. The midweek traffic was light and Pete's only concern in the world was how to kill the next few hours with so few dollars in his pocket.

"Hey, lookie, LeRoy. What'd we have here?" Pete already knew how the unattended BMW parked on the shoulder of the road could be a solution to their temporary financial bind.

"Looks like a broke down car, but I don't see no driver."

"Yeah, well, he must have hitched a ride. I'm gonna just pull up here and you load it up, but make it quick."

"Ah, Pete, do I hafta? We don't even know where the owner is?"

Pete pulled the truck up in front of the BMW and backed into position. He reached across, caught both of LeRoy's overall shoulder straps in his big hairy hand and twisted them together until LeRoy began to choke and drool brown spittle. "I said, make it quick. We got business to take care of."

LeRoy gasped for breath and wiped his mouth with the sleeve of his shirt when Pete released his grip. His bottom lip shot out like a pouting child's as he threw open the truck's rusty door and jumped down. He didn't dare talk back to Pete, but he spit tobacco juice, mumbled angrily, and kicked the dirt as he approached the abandoned car.

Moments later, they had the BMW loaded and were off for a side trip to their friends in the desert who specialized in used cars. Pete counted it good fortune that the BMW was so close to the turn-off and away from the curious eyes of the highway patrol. It didn't take long before they turned off the main highway and found themselves bouncing along on a road laced with potholes and cracks caused by the heat of the desert sun.

Pete was mentally counting the cash he hoped to get in exchange for the car, but LeRoy continued to pout. The truck banged and clanked noisily along the rough road, and conversation would have been difficult.

"Why'd ya try to choke me, Pete?" LeRoy shouted.

Pete chuckled. "Ah, I wasn't tryin' to choke ya. Just needed to get your attention."

"Ya choked me, hard! I hate when ya do that!" LeRoy hung his head like a puppy who'd just been scolded.

"Next time I tell ya to do somethin,' don't be wastin' time askin' stupid questions and sayin' dumb stuff."

LeRoy kept his head down and concentrated on the dust particles that whirled in through the open window and settled on his overalls and everywhere else. Pete looked over and wondered how long he'd stay silent.

Ten minutes went by before LeRoy turned to Pete, "Can I just say one thing?"

"Sure," Pete replied.

"Why don't we just leave this broken down old truck, hot wire the car, and go to Vegas in style?"

Pete jammed on the brakes and they skidded to a dusty stop. "Okay, by golly, LeRoy, let's do it." He thought for a minute about the ramifications. "Of course, we still don't have no cash, but the ransom money will fix that problem. Let's see what we got here."

The two men excitedly clamored down from the tow truck and began to inspect the BMW. It was locked, but Pete was an expert with a slim jim, and it was open before he broke a sweat. They slid inside with Pete in the driver's side as usual. The camel colored leather upholstery smelled like new. There were two cameras, several maps, a suitcase with women's clothing, and a make-up kit. Inside one pocket of the make-up kit was a plastic folder with credit cards for Costco,

Sears, May Company, Visa, and Mobile. They jumped out and rolled the car off the truck.

"Whooey, we've struck it rich!" Pete got out of the car and left the driver's door open. "LeRoy, you just wiggle yourself under that dash and fire this thing up so we can be on our way."

LeRoy slid across to the driver's side, but he hesitated. Leaning toward the open door, he said, "Are you sure a guy who is always sayin' 'dumb stuff' can get this car a-goin'?" He waited for a reply.

"LeRoy, you don't always say dumb stuff."

"You said not to waste time sayin' dumb stuff. Do you think my idea to swap vehicles was dumb stuff?"

"Look, LeRoy, let's just get on the road."

"I wanna know. Was my idea dumb stuff?"

"No, your idea was not dumb stuff. So let's get goin'. You're wastin' time."

"I'm not startin' the car until you say my idea was a good idea." LeRoy crossed his arms across his skinny body and looked straight ahead.

Pete knew he could start the car himself, but it would be a chore to bend his fat body into the necessary position to reach the wires. That job was so much better suited for LeRoy. "Okay, LeRoy, you win. Start the car."

"I ain't startin' her up until you say it was a good idea." LeRoy didn't move.

"I can start the darned car without you, LeRoy."

"Say it!"

Pete leaned against the car and wiped the sweat from his forehead. The only sign of life in any direction was sagebrush, a lizard that skittered under the shade of the car, and the highway they would soon leave far behind.

"Okay, LeRoy. Your idea was a good one."

LeRoy went to work with the hint of a smile on his dirty face. It didn't take him long to get the engine running. They switched places, Pete turned the car around and they headed back toward the highway. The gas gage registered nearly empty, but Pete hoped they could make it to one of the few stations on the way to Las Vegas.

CHAPTER 12

Sergeant Childers had half expected to hear back from his Uncle John, but he didn't. Instead, there was a message from a Winston Rydell who urgently wanted to speak to him. He punched in the number and waited.

"Hello?" A raspy voice crackled.

"This is Sgt. Childers of the San Bernardino Sheriff's Department. Are you Winston Rydell?"

"Yes…I'm Winston. They call me Winner."

"Okay, Mr. Rydell…Winner…how can I help you?"

There was a long pause and Childers had a feeling the caller was considering hanging up. "Mr.…I mean Winner. Are you there?"

"Yeah, sure, I'm here," Winner replied.

"Is there something I can do for you?"

The caller cleared his throat and took a slow breath. "About that reward. What would determine who got it?"

"I assume you're talking about the reward offered for information about Grace Partain?"

"Yeah."

"Well, if someone called and had some clues that would help us find her and bring her home safely, that person would certainly get the reward or part of it."

"Part of it?"

"They might have to share with other people who had additional information along the way."

"How could the person be sure of getting the reward after the whole thing was over?"

"That's our job. Look, Mr...I mean, Winner. Do you have information or not?"

Childers was usually quite patient, but this cat and mouse conversation wasn't going anywhere and he had better things to do. He drummed his fingers on the counter and was ready to hang up.

"I think so."

"You think so? Well, shoot. What do you know?"

Again there was a long pause. Childers was working up a sweat and wished he was within arm's reach of this Winner guy so he could speed up the process.

"You come on over to Henderson. I'll meet you at the Double-Up Bar around seven. Bring something to write on, and we'll talk."

"Something to write on?" But the line was already dead. The call was over just when Childers was hoping it would continue. Was this guy pulling his leg or did he really have something? But Childers didn't see that he had much choice. He would have to show up at the Double-Up Bar to find out. Meanwhile, he was going into town to watch his oldest boy, Ronnie, play catcher in a T-ball game. The timing would be just right to allow him to see most of the innings before he took off for Henderson. He tried hard to be at every game even when he was on duty. If he got lucky and there were no calls from the dispatcher, he sometimes made it all the way through the game. He knew Ronnie was thrilled either way to have his dad drive up in the white sheriff's car.

By five o'clock, Grace began to stir. The rest she desperately needed had been intermittently interrupted by snippets of nightmares that included Madeline coming toward her with the broom. She would jump violently every time the handle came down across her face. The lumpy sofa had given her a stiff neck, but Grace was grateful for the safety of Sadie's apartment. She felt the bandage on her forehead to convince herself that what happened had been more than just a nightmare. There was a throbbing pain now that the numbness from the sedative was wearing off. Grace sat up and stretched gingerly.

"Sleeping Beauty has decided to wake up?" Sadie entered the living room. Her clothes were wrinkled, her hair disheveled, but she was smiling—as always. She sank into the rocker next to the sofa.

"Sleeping Beauty doesn't feel too beautiful. Can I freshen up in your bathroom?"

"Sure! Gloria, I brought your bag of stuff in. I'll get it." Sadie jumped up, leaving the rocker rocking, and headed for the door. She scooped up the bag and deposited it in Grace's lap. "There you go."

"First of all, my real name is Grace."

"Huh?" Sadie frowned and fell back into the rocker.

"Call me Grace. I'll tell you more when I get a new face on."

"To go with your new name...Grace? I'm anxious to hear about this."

"Actually, you are *'eager,'* not 'anxious,' to hear about this. Anxious means worried. Eager means looking forward to. Sorry, I'm a school teacher, too."

Grace disappeared into the bathroom, leaving Sadie to puzzle over the mystery.

At the sink, Grace experienced a shock. Staring back at her in the mirror was a face that was almost unrecognizable as being her own. The bandage on her forehead didn't come as a surprise, but the swollen lip and blackened cheek with traces of bloody paths that were not completely washed away made her look like a victim one might see pictured on TV after an accident. Streaks of blood decorated her shirt and her hair looked as though it hadn't been brushed or curled for days. This was not the same professionally coifed, perfectly made-up, precisely dressed woman who left home just four days earlier. No amount of makeup could cover the remains of her beating.

She bathed her face with a washcloth soaked in cool water. The relief was instant and temporary, but she enjoyed it and let the excess water run down her arms. She gingerly applied cold cream over her face and neck and cleansed it away. Then slowly and carefully Grace applied her makeup, wincing with pain and knowing full well she would never be able to cover up the damage.

Back in the living room, she tried to smile, but her swollen lip pulled to the left, giving her a twisted look. She put her hands up to cover her face. "Why didn't you tell me I looked like the monster from the Black Lagoon? What a mess I am."

Sadie gave her a sympathetic smile. "Well, you certainly don't look like you did two days ago, but you were Gloria then. What did you start to tell me about the name?"

Grace sat down at the kitchen table hoping Sadie would fix something for them to eat. She was starved and she knew it would take some time to tell the story about her disappearance. Sadie took the hint and went right to work fixing macaroni and cheese out of a box.

"This all started when the turnaround bus I was supposed to be on crashed in a dust storm on the desert."

"I heard something about that wreck, but why would that cause you to change your name?"

Grace told the whole story. By the time she was finished, tears streaked her newly made-up face. "I was just so tired of being alone. Phil was tied up in his business and hardly noticed me. I've been feeling lousy lately and it just finally got to me. When the bus crashed and everyone thought I was missing, I decided it would be a good chance to change my identity and stay missing."

"Wow! Weren't you afraid?" Sadie's eyes were wide with amazement.

"Not really. It just seemed like I was playing make-believe and going along with whatever happened."

"Do you and Phil have kids?" Sadie was cutting up vegetables for a salad, but she listened intently.

Grace dropped her head. "No, I think that was our whole problem. We never had children to tie us together...to make us a family."

"Did you want them?"

"I did, but Phil never agreed. He was too busy working. He's a good man, but we just got farther and farther apart."

"Does he love you?" Sadie asked.

"Hmm. I don't know. Maybe...but he's forgotten how, I think."

Sadie put the knife down and brushed her red hair back with her wrist. "Glor...I mean Grace, I wish I had a husband who loved me. I wouldn't run away. I'd knock myself out to please him."

Grace pondered the statement. "I haven't knocked myself out for him in a long, long time. I think I gave up."

"Well, I have a little secret, too." Sadie grinned. "I hope you won't think I'm terrible, but I'm pregnant...and I'd give anything to have a husband that loved me to share this child with."

"Oh, Sadie. I don't know what to say. Should I be happy for you?"

"I know it doesn't seem right to be a single mom, but I didn't have a choice."

"Do you want to tell me about it?"

"In a minute."

Sadie set the table quickly. She served ice water, salad, and the cheesy macaroni. Grace was starved and felt so fortunate to be safely here with Sadie. She drank half of the cold water and started on the salad with her fork.

Sadie touched her hand.

"Could we pray before we eat?"

Before Grace could respond, Sadie bowed her head and began. "Jesus, thank you for Grace. Thank you for this food and the ability to earn it. Bless it to the nourishment of our bodies and help us figure out what to do next. Amen."

They both sat quietly for a few moments. When Sadie picked up her fork, Grace took a small bite of the macaroni.

"Two years ago, I got kicked out of my parents' home because I got involved with drugs. I was hanging around with a bunch of bad kids that partied constantly. Actually, when I think about it now, it makes me sick to think of what we did as 'partying.' Anyway, about four months ago, I found out I was pregnant. My life was a mess, I couldn't go home, and I didn't know what to do. I didn't have any money to go to the doctor or get an abortion or anything."

"Would you have gotten an abortion?" Grace interrupted.

"I don't know. I was pretty hopeless at the time. Anyway, this guy came into the casino telling people that Jesus loved them and handing out little brochures. Of course, the bouncer threw him out of there, but I hung on to the brochure and called the guy."

"What did he say you should do?"

"It wasn't like that. His name was Scott and he just listened to my story. Then he prayed...over the phone! It seemed crazy, but he started coming over to show me things in the Bible and to pray with me. He was so nice to me even though some nights I was stoned. He told me Jesus died for me even though I was a mess. He said Jesus paid the price for me to live eternally in Heaven and all I had to do was accept Jesus as my Lord and Savior and He would forgive all my sins."

"Was he trying to get you to go to his church or buy some books?"

"No. He invited me a couple of times, but he said every person has to make a decision about Christ: to serve him or to serve Satan. Whew! It seemed so simple. I sure didn't want to go to hell with Satan even if my life seemed like a living hell."

"So what happened?" Grace had eaten her salad, but every time she started to her mouth with a bite of macaroni, she got more engrossed in the story and asked more questions.

"One night, I prayed with him and asked Jesus to come into my heart and forgive me. It was amazing and wonderful. Suddenly, I knew my soul was satisfied. The emptiness was filled and all I could think about was learning more about Jesus."

"What about the drugs?"

"The Lord filled me up with joy and all of a sudden, I didn't want the drugs anymore. I didn't want to give myself to the devil anymore. Scott prayed for me to have strength and to be delivered, and I was."

"So where is Scott now?"

"He was taking a bunch of kids home from youth group one night. A carload of hoodlums started following them. At one point, they rammed the back of his car for no reason. When he got out to see if he could talk to them, they shot him!" Sadie burst into tears and wiped her eyes with her napkin.

"Shot him? That's terrible. Oh, Sadie, I'm so sorry."

"He died the next morning in the hospital, and I was right there with him. I loved him so much and he loved me. He was willing to accept this baby as his own and was already talking about marriage."

Grace thought about how she would have felt if Phil had ever been taken away from her. They, too, were terribly in love in the start. How had they let that love slip away from them? They had so much going for them, so much potential that they had never taken time to cultivate together. Grace grieved the loss of their relationship as she grieved Sadie's loss of her loved one.

"I'm so sorry, Sadie. What will you do now?"

"I have a lot of friends at the church where Scott and I went. They are wonderful and the Lord has done so much in my life in the past few months, I can't even begin to tell you. I know his plan for me is perfect, and I look forward to what he has in store for me."

"Sounds like your faith is strong." Grace figured when Sadie gave her the Bible that she was some sort of religious fanatic. But listening to Sadie describe how her life had been changed was a testimony nobody could argue with. "But how will you care for the baby?"

"Now, that's a problem, but I know God's hand is in it. I think after last night, I probably don't have a job at the casino anymore, which is probably a blessing in disguise. But I only have about twelve more weeks to go before delivery."

Grace was already wondering how Phil would feel about her coming home with an expectant mother to care for. She really needed to find out how Phil would feel about her coming home at all, after pulling this awful stunt and nearly getting herself killed. She needed him more than she had thought. Even though he hadn't spent much time with her in the past few years, she realized he had always been faithful and never would have let anything happen to her. He had given her security when she'd needed affection. Staying in Las Vegas was out of the question. Madeline was dangerous and there was no telling what she had told Jerry by this time.

"Sadie, may I use your phone to call Phil? It's time to tell him where I am and see if he'll come and get me. Let's cross one bridge at a time." She felt stimulated by a burst of new energy and excitement for life. There was so much she had to tell Phil.

Sadie handed the cordless phone to her and she didn't hesitate to punch in the number. The phone rang three times and the message machine answered. She hung up.

"Why didn't you leave a message?" Sadie asked.

"I don't know. I didn't know what to say." She stared at the phone and then she tried again. When the announcement was over, she said, "Hello Phil, it's Grace. I want to come home. I'll call again later." She left Sadie's number before hanging up.

Before Grace could breathe a sigh of relief, she suddenly felt nauseous. She pushed back the chair to leave the table and started running for the bathroom, but the attack was too violent and she stumbled toward the sink, vomiting across the counter uncontrollably.

Ronnie Childers hit a home run in the third inning and every player came off the bench to pound his helmet, give him a high five and a punch on the arm. There was pandemonium as the winning run was marked on the score board and Ronnie kept running right off the field and into his dad's waiting arms. Childers lifted him off the ground in a grand hug and kissed his cheek proudly. "Congratulations, son. What a great hit! What a game!"

"Thanks, Dad. Thanks for staying to the end. Could we go out for a hamburger or something?"

Childers had been nervously watching the time. Now he would really have to push it to make it to Henderson on time and meet the mystery witness.

"Ronnie, I'm sorry, but I've got to run. Tell your mom I had to go to Henderson and it might be a late night. Here's some money. You take her and your brother out to celebrate, would you?"

"Ron—nie! Ron—nie! Ron—nie!" family and friends called out.

"Guess I better go, Dad. Thanks again for being here. See you later." Ronnie ran back to his team and his waiting fans.

Childers didn't waste any time. He raced out to the highway and headed toward Henderson.

It was mid-afternoon when Troude went home to tell his wife about their trip to Las Vegas. Phil stayed home to get the money ready to go. He wanted to stay close to the phone as long as possible.

He stacked the packets of money in a suitcase ready for transport. He thought about putting blank pieces of paper in between the bills like he'd seen on TV movies, but in his mind's eye, he could see the irate kidnappers discovering the trick and shooting them all. He wished Ralph Moore had called back with some encouraging information...or at least called back. Phil wondered if he was hot on their trail and unable to make contact. Just in case, he quickly prayed for Moore's safety and that he would make the rendezvous at ten o'clock.

The suitcase full of bills weighed more than Phil expected. He shifted it from one hand to the other, but with considerable effort. He thought about putting the money in two suitcases, but decided to stick with one bag, leaving one hand free for action.

Later, at the Troude's, the men agreed to stop in at the San Bernardino Substation in Baker and tell the pastor's nephew, Sergeant Childers, the truth about the kidnapping and enlist his help. It was the only way Mrs. Troude would agree to "the mission" as she called it. She wasn't thrilled about her husband's insistence on being involved, but agreed to pray for their safety and wait for their speedy return. Pastor Troude reassured her that their nephew Tom would be with them, and he had the authority of the law. He was feeling quite adventurous and excited about being part of the capture of these scoundrels and the rescue of Mrs. Partain.

From Highland to Baker, their conversation vacillated between discussions of God to their ensuing meeting with the criminal...or criminals.

Phil looked from the road to Troude. "It just dawned on me that I've assumed all along there is only one kidnapper because I only heard one voice, but shoot, it could be more." The idea sent a shudder through him.

"Yes, for this kind of money, it could be a whole kidnapping ring. A half a million is pretty high stakes."

Troude asked a number of questions about Grace and her disappearance. He wanted to know every detail that might help them. He considered himself to be brave in the face of danger, but he had never been involved in something quite so perilous.

When they reached Baker, the deputy on duty at the station told them Childers had gone to Henderson. "Can you radio him?" Phil asked.

"Sure, but he's out of his vehicle right now after some guys in a stolen car. He doesn't have any backup yet, so…What do you want me to tell him when he's got things under control there?"

"Tell him we're going to get Grace Partain and to meet us at the Full House Casino in Las Vegas at ten tonight."

"Will do. I'll let him know."

Childers pulled off behind the BMW. The two men were already out of the car, but they didn't look like BMW owners. Overalls, work boots and caps told another story. Childers ran the plates and saw the owner was a woman in Bakersfield. The men seemed dumbfounded at first. Then the fat one pulled off his cap and slapped the skinny one across the head with it, but they didn't make any moves toward the sheriff's car. Childers called in his find, but too many miles separated him from any backup for a while. He'd have to handle this himself.

"Hello, boys. What's the problem here?" Childers approached. He unsnapped his holster, but did not draw his gun.

Pete swung his cap toward LeRoy's head again, but LeRoy put his arms up and ducked away. "This darned fool forgot to fill up the gas tank."

"Outa gas, huh?"

LeRoy started jabbering incoherently. "I told him we should'na taken…"

Pete slapped LeRoy on the side of the head. "Should'na taken the car out with no gas. You're the dummy who said we…Oh, never mind."

Childers peered into the back seat and saw women's clothing, an overnight case that hung open, and a camera. He wondered why they hadn't run when they saw him. The fat one didn't look like he'd make it very far in the desert, and the skinny one was too scared.

"Where were you headed?"

"Vegas."

There was always a chance the two of them could overpower him. They seemed pretty harmless, but they might be stupid enough to try it.

"Hmm. How about me giving you a ride? I'm headed that way."

Pete knew they only had about twelve dollars between them. They had to get to the Full House before ten or a half a million dollars would be lost.

"I guess that'll work. We got business to attend to."

"Why don't you lock up your car. You can bring gas back on your way home."

"Sure." Pete made an irritated face at LeRoy as he used the inside automatic lock to lock the doors. He'd left the slim jim back on the tow truck, so reentry would be a problem. As they shuffled toward the sheriff's car, LeRoy mumbled to Pete, "Ya suppose we coulda siphoned some gas out of the tow truck?" At that, Pete kicked LeRoy in the rear end and sent him stumbling through the dust.

Childers opened the back door to his car and stood out of the way to afford them entrance. They slid in like two little boys thrilled with the prospect of taking a ride in a police car. When the door was securely locked, Childers asked their names, asked for their drivers licenses, and then read them their rights. It was too easy and he chuckled at how everyone would laugh at how he apprehended them. He was going to have to step on it to get to Henderson by seven, so his captors would just have to ride along. They were safe and sound in the back. LeRoy whimpered while Pete berated him for suggesting they steal the car in the first place.

"You always come up with the dumbest ideas!" Pete snapped.

When Moore had interrogated Jerry and Madeline thoroughly, he still wasn't sure what he had. He knew this Gloria person might be Grace even though she didn't match up in any way to the description he'd been given. He knew Jerry had met him at the door with a gun and was unwilling to explain what that was about. And both Jerry and Madeline were very careful about every answer they gave. Moore suspected they were up to something besides playing hide-and-seek with Gloria. It was time to move ahead.

"Where do you think we might find Gloria or Grace if she's one in the same?"

Jerry hesitated. He was confused himself. Did he want to help Moore find Grace in hopes of getting the $50,000 reward or did he want to keep her whereabouts secret until he could get to her and recover the dope? The reward was larger, but how long would it take to get it? If he didn't come through with the coke for Vito, he could be dead before he ever got the reward.

"There's a girl at work named Sadie. She and Gloria seemed to be kinda friends. I'm thinking maybe she went somewhere with Sadie."

"This Sadie, where could we find her?" Again, Moore felt he was making progress.

Jerry made a sudden move and Moore jumped to his feet, his hand sliding in under his light jacket to locate his handgun.

"Hey, wait a second. I was just getting my wallet. I...I've got Sadie's phone number." Moore slowly sat down, hiked up his pants a bit and settled back on the chair.

"Got an address?"

"No. She had an old boyfriend who showed up once in a while and she didn't want anyone knowing where she lived for fear they'd tell him and he'd find her. Want me to call?"

"Yeah. See if she knows where Glor...Grace is. Ask for the address. If she knows where she is, maybe we can meet somewhere."

Jerry picked up the phone and dialed the number. "Hello, Sadie, Jerry here. You left in a hurry last night. I was a little worried about Gloria collapsing in the casino. Do you have any idea where she might be?"

There was some back and forth conversation that didn't sound too promising. "Okay, I'll see you there, but if you know where to get hold of Gloria, you better bring her down there with you. Some pretty important people are looking for her." Jerry hung up with a smirk.

"So?" Moore wished he'd asked to listen in on another phone. He hated having to depend on Jerry.

"Sadie says she doesn't know where Gloria went. She says she (Sadie) is coming in to work tonight as usual. Of course, today is payday, so it figures. You heard what I told her, but just don't forget I'm the guy who put you on to her. I'm the guy whose name goes on that reward check."

CHAPTER 13

Grace lay on the sofa with a cool towel on the part of her forehead that wasn't covered with the bandage. She was pale and her once perfect hair stuck to her sweaty face. Sadie finished cleaning up the mess without retching herself, and joined Grace in the living room.

"Gee, I didn't think my cooking was that bad," Sadie said, only half-joking.

"*Oooh*, Sadie. What *is* going on?" Grace's voice was barely a whisper. "I've never felt this sick."

"I don't know, but that's about the way I started out this pregnancy."

Grace yanked the compress away from her head and winced with pain. "Ooh! Now, there's something I hadn't thought of," she chuckled slightly, but even that hurt.

"Well?" Sadie waited for a response.

"Do you realize I've been married almost twenty years? I used to think about getting pregnant without Phil's approval, but decided that was not right and gave up the idea. After a while, I got careless about birth control and nothing ever happened, so I just figured it wasn't meant to be."

Sadie got up and walked into the bathroom for a few seconds. There was the sound of cabinets opening and closing, then she returned. "What would you say if I told you I've got a home pregnancy test kit in the bathroom? Would you like to check it?"

"You're joking, aren't you?"

"No. I'm betting you're pregnant," Sadie grinned.

Grace waved both hands as if to cancel out that idea. "I'm sure this has something to do with menopause."

"Can't hurt to check. I never heard of puking as one of the menopausal symptoms, but what do I know?"

Grace was reeling. The idea of being pregnant on top of all the other mess she'd gotten herself into was more than she could fathom. Her curiosity was stronger than her desire to just lie still and try to keep the room from spinning. She made her way to the bathroom.

The phone rang and Sadie was glad for the distraction. It was Jerry asking about Gloria. She denied knowing Gloria's whereabouts, but agreed to be at work at the usual time. He hadn't asked her about Grace, so technically, she had told the truth.

❦

Phil and Pastor Troude stopped to have dinner outside Las Vegas at a Denny's. It was easy to access without getting caught up in the casino traffic. After their side trip to the Baker Sheriff's Department, most of their conversation had focused on how they should approach the kidnappers. Phil had almost forgotten about Ralph Moore being on the case since he'd never heard from him again. He could only wonder about his progress and hope that he would show up behind the Full House at the appointed time. Whether he had found more information about Grace or not, he had to be there. If there was a showdown, Ralph was the only one with authority—or a gun.

Inside the restaurant, they hardly noticed the other customers as they continued their conversation. "I'll carry the suitcase full of money," Phil said, "and we'll approach from opposite ends of the building. That way we'll have more of a chance to see what's going on, get license numbers, give them more than one moving target, and…what am I talking about? I can't put you in a situation where you might get killed. What if they have guns? What if they don't even bring Grace along? What if Grace is dead?" Phil was working himself into a sweat.

"Calm down, Phil. We've got to pray and have faith that God will be with us. Giving him your heart is only the beginning of walking with him. Jesus said, 'I will never leave you or forsake you.' Now your faith will be tested in a real way."

"Are you telling me not to make a plan?" Phil was scared and frustrated. He had so many questions to ask when Grace was safely back in his arms.

"Not at all. We should have a plan, but be flexible because God may change that plan in a way you never imagined. Did you ever hear about the parting of the Red Sea?" Troude smiled knowingly.

"Of course, but I honestly didn't think that applied to this day and age." Phil remembered his grandmother telling him the story about Moses, but he had always thought of it as a fairy tale for a young boy.

"God is the same yesterday, today, and forever. He's no less powerful today than in the past."

Phil thought about programs he'd seen on TV and newspaper stories he'd read about people being miraculously healed or saved from perilous danger. He hadn't thought about giving God the credit, but it was always a mystery how such things happened.

"I guess that's our only hope." Phil settled down.

"I *know* that's our GREAT hope. God is my rock, in him will I trust."

Phil's frown turned to a partial smile. "How do you always know just the right thing to say?"

"I don't, but God does. He is everything we need and his Word is as powerful as a sword. I read it over and over to know him better, and he has never let me down."

The waitress smiled as she sat their salads down in front of them. Troude, forever concerned about fitness, had ordered his light dressing on the side. Phil, continuously on the run, gave no thought to diet and his salad was slathered with blue cheese dressing.

Troude thanked the waitress and almost immediately bowed his head and thanked God. At the same time, he asked protection for himself and Phil and prayed to find Grace alive. He asked that God's will be done and asked for blessing on the food and its preparers. Phil bowed his head, but he felt strange and a bit embarrassed.

"Amen," Troude concluded.

Phil picked up his fork, but waited while Troude carefully selected the first morsel of lettuce and barely touched it to the dressing.

"Do you always do that?" Phil asked.

"What?"

"Pray before eating…and in public?" Phil stuck a clump of lettuce dripping with dressing into his mouth.

"Absolutely. I thank God for everything I have, just the way I thank the waitress for bringing it to the table. And as for whether it's public or private, do you want to be blessed by God in public or only in private?"

Phil pondered the question. "I think I'd like to be blessed by him everywhere."

"Then you can't be ashamed to bring him into public with you. How would a best friend feel if you were ashamed to bring him into public or introduce him to your friends?"

"Wow. I never thought of Jesus in that way…I mean, as a best friend. Hmm."

"You will, as you learn to live your life knowing he is always with you."

"Wow," Phil felt like he was a whole new person and he was seeing God for the first time.

Sergeant Childers pulled up in front of the Double-Up Bar. He had called ahead to ask that one of the Henderson sheriffs meet him there. He couldn't leave Pete and LeRoy in the car unattended; it wasn't good practice. With the automatic locks on the back doors and the steel divider between the front and backseat, they weren't going anywhere. He knew they were secure, but he was already nervous about taking them across the state line on this escapade. The Henderson deputy was there as promised, waiting in his car. Childers got out of the car and introduced himself. "I sure appreciate this. These two characters are probably going to be okay, but I didn't want to take any chances."

"I'll just sit in your car with the AC on until you come back. No sense having both our cars running."

The heat outside was intense. "I hope you can stand the smell of these guys," said Childers. "They're pretty ripe. I'll try to make this interview as quick as possible."

He walked back to the car. "Okay, boys. You stay put for a while and I'll leave the air-conditioning on. A deputy will keep you company." He remembered the voice telling him to bring something to write on. Reaching across the seat, he pulled out his metal clipboard and got out just as the other deputy came to stand watch. Through the metal divider, he could see Pete and LeRoy waving their arms in a flurry of weak attacks and wondered how long they'd be safe together...not from escape but from each other.

"Hey, you two. Calm down back there or I'll have to put handcuffs on you," the deputy warned. He was young and new on the department. It had been a quiet day, and he jumped at the chance to take this call for help. Now he was wondering about the wisdom of his decision.

They quieted down temporarily.

Childers looked back briefly and entered the bar. It was just 7:00 p.m. and besides the few people scattered here and there, only one guy seemed to be alone. He was sitting in a booth back in a corner, but in full view of the front door. Childers held up the tablet and the lone man signaled him back to the table.

"Winner?" Childers extended his hand when the man confirmed his identity.

Winner appeared to be about forty with leathery weatherbeaten skin. He looked like the kind of guy, Childers thought, you might see walking along the shoulder of the highway with a bedroll across his back. His eyes were sunken and bloodshot. He sat with both hands curled around an empty beer bottle.

"I can't stay long, so let's get right down to business. I've got my tablet and I'm ready to write?" Childers had his doubts about this meeting, but there was no sense wasting time.

"I heard on TV there was a reward for information about the disappearance of that lady in the bus wreck."

"Yes, fifty thousand dollars." Childers decided he was going to let Winner do all the talking. If he knew anything substantial, he'd have to be convincing without any help.

"The night of the accident, I was on the bus."

"Okay."

"I was on the return trip to San Bernardino. I've got a girlfriend there, but ever' now and then, she kicks me out."

That didn't surprise Childers. Who would want this character?

"It's free to ride the turnaround bus to Las Vegas, so once or twice a week, I take the trip. It gives her a chance to get over being mad at me."

Childers was amazed that someone would take frequent bus trips just to kill time. His memories of riding the school bus weren't filled with thoughts of comfort or leisure travel.

"It's nice and cool on the bus and they give you some gambling tokens, snacks, and a coupon for a buffet. So it makes a pretty good day when you don't have anything else to do."

"Interesting way of life. Don't you have a job?" Childers immediately regretted the question because it was irrelevant and he wanted to get this over so he could go home.

"I work in construction when I need a few bucks, but I just wasn't cut out for the routine of a regular job. Too much stress."

A sarcastic remark flitted through Childer's head, but he decided it was uncalled for and left it unsaid.

"Okay, so you take these turnaround trips regularly."

"When I'm in the casinos, I pretend I'm a gambler, and when the cocktail waitress comes around, I accept all the free drinks they offer."

"Had you been drinking on the day of the accident?" Childers tried to get back on course.

"Sure. I had been drinking with some loser guy at the bar who was spilling his troubles to me. I didn't care because he was buying."

Childers scribbled some notes. "So you were on the bus, and you were drunk."

"That lady, Grace…uh, I think it's Partain…I sat down right beside her in the front seat."

Childers wrote a word or two, but didn't say anything.

"I hadn't had a bath in days, and was pretty sauced. She didn't say anything to me, but I could tell she wasn't happy about sharing a seat with me."

"Seems to me I remember that the bus wasn't full to capacity. Why did you sit in the front seat with her anyway? Weren't there other empty seats?"

"Yeah, but I enjoy the view. The front seat is the best place to see everything."

"Okay." So far, Childers was unimpressed. He thought of the four-hour trip across the desert and wondered how interesting the view could be to a drunk who made the roundtrip twice a week.

"I was next to her for only a minute when she jumped up and left the bus in a hurry. She acted weird…kind of panicked or shook up."

"Shook up?"

"Like she was sick or something. She looked a little green if you know what I mean. She kinda put her hand over her mouth."

"Did she say anything to you?"

"No. To tell you the truth, she looked like she was headed for the nearest toilet bowl. And she wasn't wasting any time. I kept my eyes closed, but she stumbled all over my feet."

"Okay. So she got off the bus."

"Yes. At first I thought she was getting off to stay, but she left her stuff rolled up in the seat."

"What stuff?" Childers was more interested.

Winner ran his finger around the lip of the bottle.

"Uh…looked like a jacket wrapped around a book and maybe her purse or something. Then…"

Winner hesitated, but Childers sat quietly with pencil poised.

"Pretty quick the driver got back on, started up the bus, and we left. I was pretty drunk. I decided she must have gone to the restroom in the back of the bus while I dozed. When twenty minutes or so passed, and she didn't show up, I decided she must have never got back to the bus or she was passed out in the bathroom. But remember, I was pretty fuzzy."

"So you're saying, Grace Partain never got on the bus for the return trip?"

"If she did, I didn't see her. If she did, wouldn't she have come up and gotten her stuff out of the seat next to me? No, I don't think she got back on that bus."

"Did you bring her absence to the attention of the driver?"

"No! Guys like me are always suspect. I wasn't about to bring it to his attention. Someone might think I did something to her. I think he counted her when she came on the bus and never saw her leave."

Childers was busily jotting notes now. "Why didn't you call me sooner?"

Winner picked up the empty beer bottle in front of him. "I don't suppose you could buy me a drink? I'm pretty dry."

"I can ask them to bring you a soda or a glass of water."

He shook his head and went on.

"It wasn't long before we hit the dust storm. Man, it was terrible. You couldn't see two feet in front of the bus." Winner's eyes seemed to revisit the scene.

"When we crashed, it was awful. The windows all busted out, and the wind was blowing dust through that bus like dirt through a vacuum cleaner." Winner breathed more quickly as the memory of the incident appeared to agitate him.

Childers interrupted. "Were you thrown out?"

"No, but some people were. I think most of them died. But inside the bus, people were tossed all over the place and everyone was screaming and crying. It was a mess." Winner made some undefined moaning sounds.

"Did you ever see Grace again?"

"I thought I did, but it wasn't on the bus."

Childers's mind was trying to make sense of this new concept. He had spent so much time looking for her in the desert it was hard to imagine that she was never there at all. "Where did you see her?"

"They took a bunch of us to the hospital. Some were dead or almost dead and some had various injuries. I got this cut from the broken glass."

He pulled back his sleeve and showed the wound on his wrist. It had been stitched up, but the area around it looked inflamed.

"Go on," Childers was eager to get to the bottom of this.

"When I was leaving the hospital a few hours later, it was already light outside, and I'm pretty sure I saw her buying a newspaper."

"In the hospital?" Childers flashed back to the doctor telling him he thought she was there.

"Yeah. And she looked just fine."

"Did you say anything to her?"

"Why would I? She didn't like my looks from the start."

Childers was trying hard to visualize this whole scene and what he would have done. "You said she left her stuff on the seat next to you. When she didn't show up, did you do anything with her things?"

Winner began to fidget. His eyes shot from Childers to the door, to the sheriff's car parked outside. "I don't know anything about the stuff in the seat."

Childers was beginning to form a better picture. "Maybe you took a peek in her purse or whatever was left there. When we found it, there were only a few items in it that identified her."

Winner started to move toward the edge of the seat, but Childers reached across and grabbed his wrist. "Where do you think you're going?"

"Gotta go to the bathroom. I'll be right back."

"I'll go with you. I've been on the road a while and we may be spending some time together."

"What do you mean?" Winner tried to wrench his hand away, but Childers held fast.

"Did you take money out of Grace Partain's purse?" He let loose of Winner's wrist.

"Listen, I called to give you some information. This isn't about me. This is about that missing lady."

"Did you take the money out of her purse? If I'm going to get the story, I want the whole story."

"That's all I'm saying. If it helps find her, then I want the reward…or at least part of it."

"You aren't getting anything, Winner. I've already traced her to the hospital, and your information didn't get me any farther."

Childers was surprised he hadn't heard anything from the dispatcher in a while. He looked down and realized he'd inadvertently turned off his radio at some point. He called in quickly to see what he'd missed. The deputy on duty told him about Uncle Troude coming through and his urgent message to meet at ten at the Full House Casino.

Winner got up from the table and headed toward the restroom.

"Where do you think you're going?" Childers asked.

"I'll be back in a minute."

As soon as Childers finished transmitting, he headed for the restroom also. Winner was half way out the window when Childers grabbed the leg of his camouflage pants and pulled him back.

"You are much too anxious to get away…and not through the front door like most people." He pulled out his handcuffs and put them on Winner. "Now let's get out of here. I've got another meeting to make and it looks like you'll just have to ride along." Childers used the facilities and escorted Winner out of the bar.

The young deputy seemed eager to get back to his own vehicle. Standing watch on Pete and LeRoy hadn't satisfied his need for excitement. It was too hot to stand outside the car and too smelly to be comfortable inside with them. He waited just long enough to see Childers help Winner into the backseat with the other two occupants. It was a bit of a squeeze with Pete taking up more than half of the plastic-covered seat.

Childers turned to thank the deputy, but he was already in his car, backing away from the bar. With a nod of his head, he sped away as if responding to an all-points bulletin.

"Hey, who's this loser?" Pete said as Childers closed the door, pushing the three men together. "How come he has to sit back here? Hey, let me sit up front."

It appeared to Childers that he had accidently gathered in two car thieves and a vagrant who had stolen money from the missing woman who wasn't where everyone thought she was. The Full House Casino would be his next stop, but he felt like he already had a full house of his own. He worried that his Uncle John had gone too far in helping Phil Partain…and what would he be doing behind a cheap casino like the Full House? For that matter, what was he doing transporting these three two-bit criminals into Las Vegas? It was getting late and he would have to hurry to make it in time. He wished he'd just left them in the deputy's custody for a few hours, but it was too late now.

Grace opened the bathroom door, but didn't move toward Sadie, who was in full view from the dining area of the small apartment. A blank look was turning into a silly grin.

"Well?" Sadie almost shouted.

Tears begin to fill Grace's eyes. "Well?" She choked back a sob. "If home pregnancy tests are the least bit accurate, I guess you were right."

Sadie squealed as she bounded across the room and threw her arms around Grace. "I told you. I told you! You're going to be a mommy!" Sadie danced around, but Grace wasn't up to dancing. She just stood there, numb with shock. For months, she thought she was entering menopause, which was the cause of her unpredictable nausea, fainting spells, and depression. How was she going to break the news to Phil? He wasn't in favor when they were young and now, here she was, forty!

"Oh my gosh, Sadie. Today is my fortieth birthday," she said, dazedly.

"What a birthday present," Sadie replied, grinning gleefully.

Maybe Phil wouldn't want her back after this crazy charade. Worst of all, would he want her back pregnant?

CHAPTER 14

The sudden knocking startled Ralph Moore. As he tried to rise, he tangled with the chair he'd straddled backward. That gave Jerry just enough time to fish under the sofa for his handgun. Ralph tried to catch his balance and reach for his own firearm, but the chair scooted out from under him and he fell with a thud to the wooden floor.

Jerry was in control now, standing over Ralph with his weapon ready. "You just stay put, Mr. Moore. Madeline, see who's at the door."

Madeline didn't open the door until she was sure of the visitor's identity. "It's your mom. Come on in, Isabel."

Isabel entered timidly. Jerry was angry, "Mom, what are you doing here?"

"I got worried," Isabel was wringing her hands.

"Worried about what? You were the one who sent this guy after us, weren't you?"

"Yes, but I thought you'd find Gloria, and Moore would find you, and then I'd…I mean we'd get the reward for leading him to her."

"Great. And now that I don't know where she is, Moore suspects I did something to hurt her."

"You did send her to the hospital for stitches, didn't you, Jerry?"

"No! I didn't do anything to her. She and Madeline had a few words though." Madeline gave Jerry a furious glare.

"You rat, Jerry. She stole your…"

"Shut up, Madeline."

Ralph saw his chance to take advantage of the confusion. He was still lying on his back looking up into the barrel of the pistol. "Can I get up now?"

Jerry wasn't sure what to do from this point. "Sure…get up. But don't get any ideas." He wished he had an idea.

"Mr. Hodges. You really aren't in any kind of trouble…yet. I don't have any reason to turn you in to the police…yet. Don't do something stupid that would change that." His stiff knees made getting up from the floor a challenge and he was huffing and puffing by the time he collapsed into the flowered overstuffed chair.

Jerry was trying to figure a way to recover the missing drugs so he could complete the sale and keep the buyer from killing him, and still find Grace and collect the reward. "Madeline, you stay here with the gun and watch Moore and I'll see if I can find Gloria. I'll make sure we get that reward."

"Why should I stay here?" Madeline folded her arms across her chest with a defiant look.

"Because I'm going to share the reward money with you, and because I said to. I can't leave Mom here alone to watch him."

Isabel stood up as though she were leaving, but Jerry stepped in her way. "You stay here, too, Mom. If I don't come back here before ten, meet me at the Casino and bring Moore with you. If I haven't found Grace by then, maybe she'll show up with Sadie for her paycheck." He handed the gun to Madeline who had been pouting about being left behind, but seemed to like the idea of being in control.

Moore started to object, but then thought of the heat outside and figured having Jerry locate the supposed impostor of Gloria Franklin might be the cooler solution. How could he lose? By ten, he'd be at the casino to apprehend whoever showed up. It was almost too easy, so he settled back to wait.

As soon as Jerry was gone, Moore slipped off his shoes. "I don't suppose I could get a little snack and a cold drink?"

"May as well get him something to eat, though he sure ain't starving to death," Madeline said to Isabel, who shuffled obediently off to the kitchen.

⁂

"What am I going to tell Phil?" Grace was baffled by the whole situation. "In fact, how am I going to get home?"

Sadie offered Grace a ride back to Highland, but she couldn't leave until she got her check. In case Jerry was going to fire them both, she wanted to get whatever money was coming to her.

"Look, Sadie, I think the whole idea of going back to the casino is dangerous. I'm scared of Madeline...and Jerry."

"From the looks of your face, you have every right to be scared."

Grace wanted more than anything to get home to Phil. Things were so much different now.

Sadie ran her hands through her red curls. "I promise, I'll just run in and run out...and I'll get both checks, yours and mine."

"I don't care about mine. I just want to get out of here and back home where I belong." It had been a long day and they both shot a glance toward the clock simultaneously.

Sadie looked anxious. "I've got to have mine, my rent is already overdue."

"If you promise to make it quick, but I'm going to be hiding in the backseat of the car. I'm not taking any chances."

"Won't everything be okay if I just drive you home?"

Grace wasn't sure if changing one's identity was a crime. Or lying, or faking a disappearance, or keeping her whereabouts a secret, or deceiving her husband whom she'd promised to love for better or worse twenty years ago. It all seemed ugly and sordid now. She looked like a common brawler. Even if she got home safely, Phil would be shocked at her appearance.

"Maybe I should call the Las Vegas police and turn myself in."

"For what?" Sadie had grown fond of Grace and didn't want anyone treating her like a criminal.

"I'm not sure. But poor Phil will feel like a fool when I reappear. He'll hate me for doing this. I mean what will people think, after it was on the news and everything." Grace put her hands to her face and wiped tears from both eyes.

"It can't be that bad. I'll pray that the Lord will sort everything out and keep us safe." Much to Grace's surprise, Sadie came to her side, took her hand and knelt at her feet. "Jesus, keep us safe and direct us to do your will. Bring Grace back together with her husband and soften his heart so he'll forgive her and understand. Amen."

Grace was in awe of Sadie and her great faith. "Sadie, if we get out of Vegas okay, I'd...I'd...like to invite you to come a stay with us until the baby is born so we can help you out."

Sadie took a big breath and let it out quickly. "That's really neat, Grace, and I appreciate the offer. But you better make amends with Phil and see if he will take YOU back before you tell him he might be getting FOUR in the deal."

"Four?"

"You and your baby, me and my baby make four."

There was shouting from outside and Sadie struggled to her feet. It was a man's voice and it was coming closer.

"I'll park there if I want to! I've got business!" It was Jerry.

They could hear the manager shouting at him about parking in the driveway. Both men cursed and there were sounds of a scuffle.

"I said, I've got business here." Jerry was banging his fist on the door.

The two women were already out of the bedroom window and climbing down the fire escape. Without a word, they ran for Jerry's car that was parked in the driveway with the engine running. Sadie jumped into the driver's seat and Grace scooted into the passenger seat, slammed her door, and they were off.

Childers was almost overcome by the stench. He had stopped and put Winner up front, hoping to quiet the protests. Even though Pete was only one day out from his hospital shower, LeRoy and Winner, who was now sitting in the passenger seat hadn't seen a bar of soap for more than two weeks. Mingled with the stale smell of Winner's booze and LeRoy's tobacco even the air-conditioning on full blast couldn't cut the odor.

"Oh man, LeRoy. Look what you done!" Pete's cap had fallen on the floor in the earlier back seat tussle and LeRoy, in an effort to get rid of some of his tobacco juice, had accidently spit in it.

Pete whopped LeRoy on the head with the soggy cap. "I didn't mean to, Pete, but I was runnin' over."

"Am I going to have to listen to you two all the way?" Childers was generally good-natured and nothing rattled him, especially not these three small-time criminals. They weren't smart enough to be too dangerous.

"Git over on yer side, LeRoy, and keep your spit to yerself."

Childers couldn't help but chuckle. They were like a couple of kids. Winner, on the other hand, hadn't said anything since they got in the car and Childers felt sure he was planning something. He might have been safer locked in the backseat with the other two, but with his hands secured to his belt by handcuffs and the door locked, escape would be difficult.

"By the way, where exactly was it you two were going in Las Vegas?" Childers asked through the wire cage.

"The Full House Casino," answered Pete and LeRoy in unison.

"The Full House Casino? Well, isn't that a coincidence, that's right where we're headed."

◦⧙ɣ⧘◦

"Doesn't it strike you funny that Jerry would leave you two women here with me?" Moore prodded. He had been quite submissive, and at Madeline's bidding, Isabel had fixed him a snack consisting of left-over lasagna piled high on a paper plate with two huge pieces of garlic-buttered French bread and a Coke. It was delicious, and he wolfed it down, but now he was ready to get back into the action.

Isabel shrugged and gave Madeline a bewildered look.

"Maybe...maybe he thought he could make more progress finding Grace without us along," Madeline answered. She tried to sound convincing, but she knew Jerry was up to something. Maybe he was going to complete the drug deal without her and leave them both behind.

"So why didn't he just tie me up and take you two along with him?"

"He left us the gun to protect ourselves," Madeline snapped, waving the pistol.

"Protect yourselves from whom? You don't even know for sure if I have a gun on me."

Madeline cocked her head remembering the moment he reached inside his jacket. They had assumed he did. Why else would they have been so willing to sit and answer questions?

She moved from the sofa to the back of the overstuffed chair where Moore was sitting. As she held the gun against his neck, she slowly ran her hand from his shoulder toward his armpit where she suspected the holster would be. She was right. Before she could react,

Moore, with one hand, wrenched the pistol out of her hand causing it to fire into the floor. He grabbed her wrist with the other hand and pulled her over his shoulder and across his lap.

Madeline, trying to push free, tumbled down Ralph's legs to the floor, but he had a firm grip and twisted her hand until she was forced to sit still on the floor. She whimpered in pain, but there was no more fighting.

Moore let go, stood up, and turned so that both women were in full view. As far as he was concerned, they were of no use to him and he needed to get to the casino to intercept Jerry.

"Ladies, thank you so much for the snack. It's been lovely, but I really must be leaving now." With that, Ralph emptied the bullets out of Madeline's handgun and tossed it to her. "Be careful with that thing, someone could get hurt." He checked his watch and left the house. Time was growing short and he headed across town to the Full House. As he started his car, he noticed a lasagna stain on his tie and knew his wife would accuse him of secret outings with an Italian cook. She knew he was a closet eater, and she never stopped worrying about his health. The extra fifty pounds he carried slowed him down a bit when he was in foot pursuit, but it hadn't handicapped him a bit when Madeline tried to get his gun. He felt proud of himself for pulling that move so quickly and successfully and grinned just a little as he replayed the scene in his mind.

Phil pulled his tan Infinity into the entrance of the alley behind the Full House Casino. Pastor Troude looked at his watch by the light of the street lamps. "It looks like we're plenty early. Why don't we just sit here for a while and see what happens."

The alleyway was big enough for two cars to pass with tall buildings on both sides. The back door to the Full House was about fifty yards down in the center of the block.

"I'll pull the car as close to the building as possible and we'll see who shows up." Phil parked, rolled down the windows, and turned off the lights. Both men automatically slid down in their seats a bit and sat quietly looking straight ahead. They were amazed how light and noisy it was even in the back alley.

A car approached the driveway behind them and they slumped even lower. It went around them and pulled in behind the Full House.

"It looked like two heads," Troude whispered.

As the driver got out and hurried toward the back door, the halogen light on the building illuminated the car's interior and they could see a passenger slumped low in the back seat.

"That looked like a woman and it looks like they belong here. They aren't waiting for anyone, and one of them had a key to enter the back." Troude was really getting into this detective business and was eager to prove himself helpful.

"I think you're right," Phil answered. "We are looking for someone who looks like they are here to meet someone...us."

A long black Lincoln entered the alley from the other end. The lights blinded them, making it impossible to see anyone in the car. The Lincoln pulled up on the opposite side of the alley in a wide spot across from the Full House back exit. The headlights went off and both Troude and Phil tried to clear their vision and readjust to the relative darkness. No doors opened. Whoever was in the car, stayed put.

"What do you think, John? Do you think those are our kidnappers?" Suddenly Phil was aware of the stupidity of his choices. He should have called the police in Las Vegas. These kidnappers were probably armed and all the money in the world wasn't going to guarantee his safety…or Pastor Troude's. What was he thinking to allow him to get involved? This wasn't a lark for an old man to relive his childhood dreams. This was serious business and lives were at stake.

They sat in silence. The flicker of a lighter illuminated at least three faces as someone in the Lincoln lit a cigarette.

"It could be them," answered Troude. "What do you think we should do now?"

"I…I guess I'll take the suitcase and walk that way. The keys are in the ignition. If everything seems to go okay, you stay put. If things go bad, get out of here and go for help."

Phil was short of breath and he could feel his heart pounding. "I sure hope this works! I'm afraid, but I've got to take the chance that they'll return Grace to me alive. I love her and I have to go through with this."

Troude put his hand on Phil's trembling shoulder. "Father God, in the name of Jesus, build a wall of protection around this man. Give him the courage to do what he has to do, the wisdom to speak the words necessary, and a sound mind to adjust to whatever happens. Have your hand on him. Now go." He gave Phil a firm pat, they shook hands, and Phil stepped out of the car.

He opened the back door and got the suitcase. "Don't quit praying, John."

"Don't worry, I won't."

Phil took two deep breaths, stood as tall as he could and stepped away from his vehicle. Headlights appeared behind him as another car entered the alley. It was a taxi and Phil jumped back inside his car.

The muffler of the taxi banged against the lip of the alley entrance as it sped by. A male passenger got out, paid the driver quickly, and turned toward the door of the Full House. Just as he got into the light, something caught his attention and he jerked around to look toward the Lincoln parked in the shadows.

There were voices from the Lincoln, but Phil couldn't make out what they were saying. Two men got out of the car, but did not make a move toward the man at the doorway. Another two emerged from the back seat of the car, and it was apparent they all had something in their hands that both Troude and Phil recognized.

"Dear God, they've got guns! Maybe they think that guy is you and they're asking him for the money." Now Troude was becoming agitated. This had turned into more than he had bargained for.

The men were shouting, demanding something, and Phil thought he heard, "…been waiting long enough." He thought they called the man Jerry, who seemed frantic now and was moving his hands as if to explain something. The driver of the Lincoln was getting impatient, shaking his gun in a threatening way and shouting obscenities. There was a shot, and at the sound, the man Phil thought was Jerry fell to his knees with his hands together in a pleading fashion.

"Oh no, is he shot?" Phil couldn't take his eyes off the scene. Troude was gripping the dash now as he strained to see the action and try to figure out what was going on. It was as though the whole kidnapping exchange was going on without them.

Headlights flashed in their rearview mirror as another car entered the alley from behind them. Suddenly, more headlights appeared, this time from the other direction. The four armed men jumped back inside the Lincoln, started the engine, and attempted to leave, but the two approaching cars pinned them in, both front and back. One was a white car clearly marked with a sheriff's department insignia on the door. The other car was driven by a stocky man in a lightweight suit who hauled his large frame out of the car with his gun already drawn. The man in the sheriff's car did the same. The stocky man trained his pistol on the kneeling man and the officer aimed his at the Lincoln.

The man on his knees fell to his face on the ground as Ralph Moore rapidly handcuffed him and then joined Childers to attend to the four men in the Lincoln, now standing in a row outside the car with their hands on their heads.

The back door to the Full House opened and Sadie came running out just in time to see the last of the men being handcuffed. She shot a glance at Jerry's car to see if Grace was still there, but the car looked empty. Sadie walked quickly to where Jerry lay face down. "What did you do with her?"

Before he could answer, Moore joined her. "Are you a friend of this guy?" Moore asked.

"Not at all," Sadie answered. "He's Jerry Hodges, the manager of this casino. He used to be my boss, but I'm getting out of here."

Moore motioned toward the Lincoln. "Do you happen to know who those guys are? One says his name is Vito."

"I don't know, but they used to hang out in the bar. I thought it had something to do with buying or selling drugs." Sadie's eyes darted from Jerry to the men and back to the car.

"Where were you going in such a hurry?" asked Moore.

"I came to pick up my paycheck. That's all."

Moore sensed that that wasn't all. "What's your name, ma'am?"

"Sadie Miller."

"You don't happen to know Grace Partain, do you?"

Jerry rolled over on his side and shouted, "Of course she does. They stole my car and now they were trying to make a getaway."

"Stole your car?" He turned again to Sadie. "Did you steal this gentleman's car?"

"We did take it and drove it here, but only because we had to. He was after us. He broke into my apartment." Sadie was beginning to cry. "We were scared to death."

Childers was busy with the four he had finished handcuffing. He didn't want to take his eyes off them for a minute and he didn't have any place to put them. Pete, LeRoy, and Winner watched the whole scene from inside the patrol car. Slowly the door of Jerry's car opened and Grace stepped out.

It was hard to tell from so far, but Phil was almost sure he recognized Grace's form. "Look! I think it's Grace...and she's alive." He threw the car door open and jumped out on the run. Troude exited the car, but stayed behind.

"Grace!" he screamed, tears of joy starting to stream down his face.

Grace smiled widely as her own tears filled her eyes. Her swollen lip split and a trickle of blood made its way down her chin. She stood shyly waiting with arms slightly opened, hoping he still cared. Phil rushed to her and held her in his arms. "Oh, thank you, God. Thank you, God. My prayers have been answered."

Phil pushed Grace out to arm's length so he could look her in the face, and he gasped. The bandage on her forehead had blood oozing through it. Her cheek was all shades of black, blue, and purple, and blood trickled from her lip. "Are you okay?"

"Yes, I'll be fine. I just want to go home." He gathered her up in his arms and held her close for a long minute or two, his face buried in her hair.

"And we are going home." He turned to Moore, who was standing close by. "Thanks so much, Ralph. I don't know what you did, but I'll be glad to pay for your services."

"But I didn't find the kidnappers."

"Kidnappers?" Grace was confused.

"Weren't they the ones who beat you up?" Phil asked.

"Kidnappers?" Grace repeated with a blank look.

"The kidnappers took you from the accident. How did you escape from them?" Now that Grace was safe, Phil wanted to make them pay for terrorizing his wife and scaring him to death.

"There were no kidnappers. I was never on the return bus. I missed it." Grace was sure Phil's attitude would change when he found out she had actually run away, but all this talk of kidnappers was a complete surprise to her.

"Who beat you up then?" Now Phil was confused.

"Madeline, another waitress in the…"

Another car was approaching. As it came closer, Phil could see two women. They stopped several feet short of the casino and got out of the car. Madeline was in the lead with Isabel trailing behind.

Jerry rolled over to see the two women. "Madeline, why did you let him go? I told you to keep him there!" he shouted.

"Let him go? You fool! He took the gun away from me."

Moore backed up so he could get Childers's attention. "Let's switch places here for a minute. You need to arrest that woman named Madeline," and he pointed toward her, "for assault on Grace Partain, and we'll figure the rest out later."

Childers calmly walked toward the group. "I believe you said your name was Madeline. Well, Madeline, you are under arrest for assaulting one Grace Partain." He reached for his handcuffs and realized his were being used by Winner right now. Madeline broke away from the crowd and ran toward her car. Childers went after her, but before he could reach the car, vehicles entered the alleyway from both directions, two on each end with sirens blaring, lights flashing, blocking Madeline's escape.

"I called the Las Vegas police when Jerry started threatening us," Sadie looked down at her shoes like a little girl who did something nobody expected.

"So did I," added Childers. "I didn't know what to expect, but I already had a car full and I knew my uncle might be in danger."

Uncle Troude grinned. "But here we all are, safe and sound. Praise the Lord."

Tom shook his uncle's hand and chuckled. "I had just discovered Grace was never on the bus when I got the call to come here. I still don't understand, but it sounds like no one else does either."

The local police officers easily corralled Madeline and then they handcuffed Vito and his men. Childers was still stuck with Pete, LeRoy, and Winner, so he decided to take them back to Baker to spend a night or two in jail. Car theft and petty thievery would be enough to detain all of them. Moore pulled Jerry to his feet and asked the Las Vegas police if they'd like another one to take along until he could press charges. They agreed, but as Jerry stumbled toward the patrol car, Isabel clutched her heart and fell writhing to the ground. "Oh, no. It's my heart. Jerry…Jerry!" she cried. "Please don't take him away. I'm dying. I need him."

Grace turned to Phil, smiled knowingly and said, "This is where I came in. Let's go home."

"Oh, Mom, knock it off. They're not going for it this time," Jerry muttered as he continued toward the car with the assistance of the officer.

At that, Isabel got up, brushed herself off and turned to go. Grace couldn't help wondering if the whole heart attack thing was a hoax in the first place. She thought of calling after Isabel and thanking her for taking her in, but that didn't seem right either. Obviously, every person there had a different idea of where she'd been for the past several days. It was going to take some time to explain it all to Phil.

"Phil, I know we have a lot to talk about. If you still want me to come home, I'm looking forward to getting started."

Phil smiled and squeezed her close again. "I want you to come home more than *anything*, more than *any time* in my life."

"I have something to tell you first." In spite of her wounded face, Phil saw her in a new light, realizing how much he loved her. He was ready for anything.

"I have something to tell you also." Phil wanted to tell her about his new life with the Lord, but he didn't want her to think he was a Jesus freak or anything.

"Phil, this is Sadie." She pulled Sadie to her side.

"Hi, Sadie." Phil shook her hand.

"She's my friend and she helped me when I needed help. Now she needs a place to stay. Could she come home with us for a while?"

Phil, concerned about a stranger coming into their life, felt uncertain. It had just been the two of them for so long. "How long a while?"

The women looked at each other. "She's pregnant and I want to help her with the baby."

Phil's brow wrinkled and he looked bewildered. "You want to bring a baby into our house? Ummm…"

"There's something else. Sadie has been telling me about the Lord and how he answers prayer."

"That was what I was going to talk to you about. I thought maybe when you got home, we could start going to church again. We have so much to learn together." Phil's heart was soaring. The whole terrible nightmare had been turned to good by a loving God who had a perfect plan for everything. It had been a real turnaround for both of them.

"Can the whole family come along?" Grace teased, not knowing how best to make the announcement.

"What do you mean? The whole family? You, me, Sadie, and her child?"

"How about you, me, Sadie, and both babies."

"She's having twins?" This was too much for Phil and his knees were beginning to feel weak.

"No, she's having one and I'm having the other." Grace wanted to shout it out, but she checked herself, hoping and praying Phil would be receptive to the idea.

"You're having a baby?" he whispered. "We're having a baby?"

"Yes," Grace whispered back.

They stood looking into each other's eyes, lips forming the kind of smiles neither of them had seen in a long time. They held each other tightly, rocking back and forth without saying a word. Sadie, with tears in her eyes, joined them in a group hug, and so did Pastor John Troude.

"I'm glad there is a happy ending," said Moore.

"It's a happy beginning," said Phil. "And by the way, happy birthday, Grace. We both had a birthday today, but I'll tell you more about that later."

"This is my last case," said Moore as he headed for his car. "I've got to get to the station and deal with those drug dealers. I'll send you a bill." As he drove by, he stuck his head out the window. "And congratulations, you two." He still hadn't identified the kidnapper and was confused about what had actually happened, but Grace didn't seem to think she'd been kidnapped, and she should know. However, she was safe and that was all that really mattered.

Childers said goodbye and wished them well. This was the first he'd heard of a kidnapper. He wondered who knew about the kidnapper and who it was if there was one. He was still puzzled by the whole case.

He dreaded the ride back to Baker with the three smelly no-accounts he had handcuffed in his car, but he was glad that Grace Partain was back with her husband, safe and sound.

Pete poked LeRoy in the ribs. They had watched the whole scene, not knowing who was who. They had never seen any of the people before and could only guess that Grace was the one with the bandage on her forehead although she hardly looked like her driver's license at this point.

"See, stupid. I told ya we'd outsmart 'em all. No one ever figgered out who the kidnappers were." Pete laughed out loud, but LeRoy didn't get it.

Leroy wondered if Childers would take Grace's driver's license away from him when they got to the jail. "I wonder who gets the reward."

Pete slapped him across the head with his soggy cap.

ABOUT THE AUTHOR

Karen Robertson is a retired teacher and administrator. After fourteen years of retirement, she was recently hired back as an adjunct Performing Arts instructor, teaching Oral Presentation Through Comedy to fifth graders.

Karen is married to her cowboy/retired firefighter husband Barry. While he is busy playing golf, team roping, and kickboxing, Karen is leading her Karen Robertson Historic Downtown Murrieta Walking Fellowship Tour. She is an inspirational speaker, Bible teacher, and standup comic.

Karen is a member of the Christian Comedy Association and recently was a finalist in the Clean Comedy Challenge at the Ice House in Pasadena, California.

She and her husband live in Wildomar, California. They have two married children and three grandchildren: Les is a senior in high school and volunteers at a facility for Alzheimer patients and is starting a Lego brick sales business with grandma (a.k.a. Gammie). He survived brain cancer when he was only four and inspired www. BRICK-BrainResearchInCancerKids.org to fund pediatric brain tumor research. Bailey is a junior. She and Gammie are writing a book about Bailey's discoveries as a young goal setter. Brady is a freshman and he excels in basketball and baseball and has played tournaments in at least six states.

Karen's first poem was published in the school newspaper when she was twelve. Her writing has included freelancing for dozens of magazines, newspapers, speech writing, authoring books, birthday jingles, comedy, and hundreds of other fun assignments.

Contact her at kanwrite@verizon.net or www.SayItWithHumor.com

CPSIA information can be obtained
at www.ICGtesting.com
Printed in the USA
FSHW02n2233260718
50700FS

9 781640 287396